Korean
Literature
Now

The Very Best Statue © Yeesookyung
Courtesy of the artist
Photo: Shin Ohseok

The Long Embrace
Literature as a microcosm of religious pluralism

Vol. 38 Winter 2017

Han Yujoo, The Impossible Fairy Tale | Jung Young Moon, Vaseline Buddha
Bae Suah, North Station | Han Kang, Greek Lessons | Ko Un, White Butterfly
Ann Goldstein, One Language

Subscribe at **KoreanLiteratureNow.com** for your free copy!

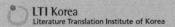
LTI Korea
Literature Translation Institute of Korea

KoreanLiteratureNow.com

GRANTA

12 Addison Avenue, London W11 4QR | email: editorial@granta.com
To subscribe go to granta.com, or call 020 8955 7011 (free phone 0500 004 033)
in the United Kingdom, 845-267-3031 (toll-free 866-438-6150) in the United States

ISSUE 142: WINTER 2018

PUBLISHER AND EDITOR	Sigrid Rausing
DEPUTY EDITOR	Rosalind Porter
POETRY EDITOR	Rachael Allen
ONLINE EDITOR	Luke Neima
ASSISTANT EDITOR	Francisco Vilhena
SENIOR DESIGNER	Daniela Silva
EDITORIAL ASSISTANTS	Eleanor Chandler, Josie Mitchell
SUBSCRIPTIONS	David Robinson
PUBLICITY	Pru Rowlandson
TO ADVERTISE CONTACT	Kate Rochester, katerochester@granta.com
FINANCE	Josephine Perez
SALES AND MARKETING	Iain Chapple, Katie Hayward
IT MANAGER	Mark Williams
PRODUCTION ASSOCIATE	Sarah Wasley
PROOFS	Katherine Fry, Jessica Kelly, Lesley Levene, Jess Porter
CONTRIBUTING EDITORS	Daniel Alarcón, Anne Carson, Mohsin Hamid, Isabel Hilton, Michael Hofmann, A.M. Homes, Janet Malcolm, Adam Nicolson, Edmund White

VOICES OF AMERICA
Robbins / Forsythe / Barton

A MIXED BILL OF NEO-CLASSICAL BALLET WITH AMERICAN INFLUENCE

12 - 21 APRIL 2018

ballet.org.uk/voices

SADL ERSW ELLS

Sadler's Wells Theatre
sadlerswells.com
020 7863 8000
⊖ Angel

LOTTERY FUNDED ARTS COUNCIL ENGLAND
Registered Charity 214005

PRAIRIE SCHOONER

BOOK
prize
series

Last year's winners

PRIZES

$3,000 and publication through the University of Nebraska Press for one book of short fiction and one book of poetry.

ELIGIBILITY

The Prairie Schooner Book Prize Series welcomes manuscripts from all writers, including non-U.S. citizens writing in English, and those who have previously published volumes of short fiction and poetry. No past or present paid employee of *Prairie Schooner* or the University of Nebraska Press or current faculty or students at the University of Nebraska will be eligible for the prizes.

JUDGING

Semi-finalists will be chosen by members of the Prairie Schooner Book Prize Series National Advisory Board. Final manuscripts will be chosen by the Editor-in-Chief, **Kwame Dawes**.

HOW TO SEND

We accept electronic submissions as well as hard copy submissions.

WHEN TO SEND

Submissions will be accepted between **January 15** and **March 15, 2018**.

For submission guidelines or to submit online, visit prairieschooner.unl.edu.

The latest volume in the acclaimed series

THE LETTERS OF
ERNEST HEMINGWAY

VOLUME 4. 1929 - 1931

EDITED BY

Sandra Spanier and
Miriam B. Mandel

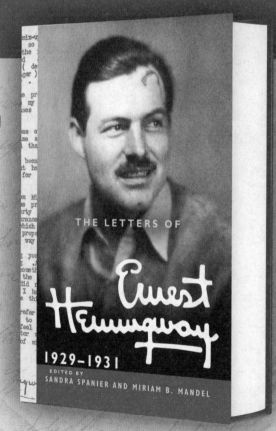

THE LETTERS OF

Ernest Hemingway

1929–1931

EDITED BY
SANDRA SPANIER AND MIRIAM B. MANDEL

Includes letters to
famous figures
of twentieth-century
literature including

F. SCOTT FITZGERALD and
JOHN DOS PASSOS

CAMBRIDGE
UNIVERSITY PRESS

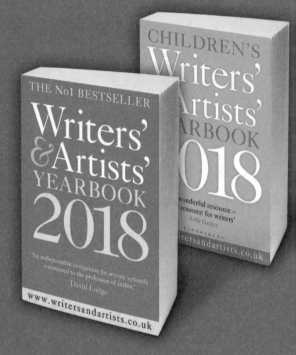

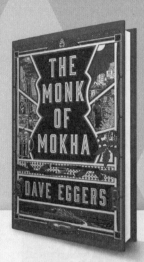

DAVE EGGERS
The Monk of Mokha

MARTIN AMIS
The Rub of Time

NED BEAUMAN
Madness is Better than Defeat

It's been a long winter...

COZY UP WITH a BOOK FROM KNOPF

HANNAH ARENDT
Thinking Without a Banister

JOHN BANVILLE
Time Pieces

PETER CAREY
A Long Way from Home

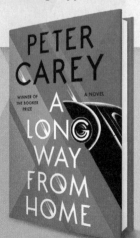

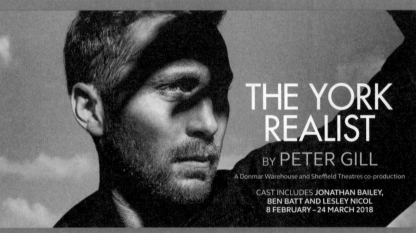
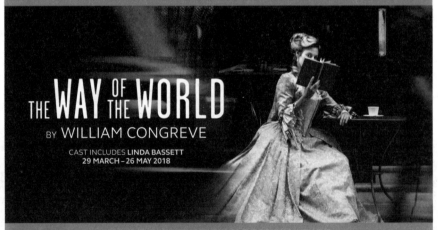

CONTENTS

Introduction

A *nimalia* is the Latin term for the animal kingdom, and the most powerful animal in that diverse group of sentient beings is *Homo sapiens*. Humans in turn have created new forms of life – or 'life' – known as robots. The term derives from the Czech *robota*, denoting drudgery or forced labour, and was coined in the 1920 play *R.U.R.* by Karel Čapek.

Some robots are builders and some are servants. The latter are still new, and tend to be gendered: the 'males' seem often designed to be small and chirpy, the 'females' to be attractive. The latter are bland machine-creatures who speak and try to understand. Like the Stepford Wives they have no emotions, we assume, but perhaps the tangles of logical thought they are capable of produce after-effects, some kind of gravel in the system which may be akin to feeling. We know where that thought goes. As Čapek wrote, 'Robots of the world! The power of man has fallen! A new world has arisen: the Rule of the Robots! March!'

Animals are rarely part of science fiction, but we live in the future now, and animals are still with us. What effect will the age of robotics have on our relationship with them? Will we still breed animals for food and for experimental purposes? Will we genetically enhance our pets? Will robots of the future be animal-based, if the inventors (and investors) can get past the ethics committees? Will we see hybrid machine life, gene-edited lambs singing in Alzheimer care homes, purring kittens kneading preset patterns on human laps, beautiful nightingales and hummingbirds switched on and off at will? We don't know – but we do know this: we are transcending *animalia*.

Our lead piece, 'The Taxidermy Museum' by Steven Dunn, is part of a longer work made up of a number of fictional interviews, mostly with soldiers, adding up to a surreal and compelling indictment of the US military machine. In this excerpt, a taxidermist explains the process of mounting the bodies of soldiers who have died in war (often, we can't help but notice, from suicide or friendly fire) in military dioramas. The distinction between humans and animals is erased, and no one really notices.

We end with Joy Williams's bleak and funny animal allegory. 'Be not afraid and be not lonely, Wilhelmina thought, but couldn't bring herself to say it. She wanted to reflect on her pretty piglets but night had fallen and she and her friends were once again hopelessly caught up in trying to comprehend the terrible ways of men.'

As are we all.

In between Dunn and Williams we have a number of dystopian and/or humorous short stories. Christina Wood Martinez writes about a mysterious astronaut landing in a small American town. Yoko Tawada describes a futuristic Japan, a poisoned world without wild animals. Cormac James's disturbing short story contemplates the destruction of marine life. Ben Lasman imagines professional rat hunters in dystopian America and Nell Zink has written an allegorical tale about immigration and incarceration.

But there is more, of course. Arnon Grunberg embeds himself in slaughterhouses in Holland and Germany, Cal Flyn goes deer stalking in the Scottish Highlands and Aman Sethi investigates rumours about village responses to a man-eating tiger on the outskirts of a nature reserve in Uttar Pradesh. Adam Foulds meditates on swifts and perspective and John Connell remembers life on a small Irish farm. We have three photoessays, poetry and some shorter pieces, too.

Most of the issue is about the transition to the future. But what if you were given a puppy, a tame evolved being, and it revealed its wild nature? Nadeem Aslam tells the story. There were moments of anger, he writes, 'something electric spilling into the air from him, his teeth bare with hate for me or for what I represented.'

What did he, and all of us, represent? Dominion over *animalia*, presumably. Displacement and destruction. ∎

Sigrid Rausing

Failure to disclose any information about
by a $10,000 fine, 5 years in prison or both.

CLEAN SLATE DISCLOSURE FORM

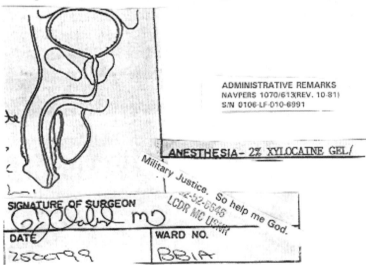

1. EDUCATION: Have you graduated
from High School? Yes(✓) No()
Have you completed any college or
vocational school? Yes() No(✓)
Have you provided transcript copies
to your recruiter? Yes() No(✓)

ADMINISTRATIVE REMARKS
NAVPERS 1070/613(REV. 10-81)
S/N 0106-LF-010-6991

ANESTHESIA- 2% XYLOCAINE GEL/

Military Justice. So help me God.
LCDR MC USNR

SIGNATURE OF SURGEON

DATE
25OCT99

WARD NO.
BB1A

THE TAXIDERMY MUSEUM

Steven Dunn

Subject Interview #03962

We lost a lot of good men over there.

Were any bad men lost?

Participation

At the Taxidermy Museum of Military Heroes we saw a bunch of people who received Medals of Honor or Purple Hearts. There was a teenage girl whose parents made her go for the same reason our Chief made us go. She said she'd stolen something from the Base Exchange and her dad said that courageous people were dying for her freedom and she was throwing away that freedom for some silly punk-rock boots.

The girl and I were standing next to a VOLUNTEERS NEEDED sign and looking at a diorama containing a taxidermied marine who'd been awarded a Purple Heart. 'When I was little, my dad told me that my grandfather had gotten a Purple Heart,' she said. 'I thought it was some type of medical condition. I imagined my grandfather's heart all swollen and turning purple until he died.'

I pointed to the sign and jokingly told her she should volunteer. 'I think my dad is gonna make me,' she said. 'For real.'

Subject Interview #80023

I am extremely proud of what I did for my country. We're the good guys, you know. I put on that uniform every morning and held my chest out and chin up, knowing I was doing some real good in the world. I know my arm won't grow back, but I have absolutely no regrets. [*Subject wipes away a tear.*] If God was willing, I would do it all over again. Yeah, all over again.

Participation

I volunteered to work at the Taxidermy Museum of Military Heroes. It gets me out of work three days a week, plus it looks like I'm taking on extra duties for my brag sheet.

Towering the expansive asphalt parking lot is the mirrored atrium, tapering to apex, giving way to sleek white facades branched into four wings, a cross. On each side of the atrium is a circle of flagpoles. On each flagpole an American flag droops halfway down. A plaque reads: THESE FLAGS WILL FOREVER BE FLOWN AT HALF-STAFF IN HONOR OF THE HEROES WHO GAVE THEIR LIFE FOR FREEDOM. Inside the circle of flagpoles is a bronze statue lying with arms out, palms to heaven, helmet cocked. Adjacent bronze rifle. Scattered bronze bullet casings.

I walk inside the atrium. Conditioned air envelops me while stained glass pools rainbows onto marble floors. In the center of the atrium, underneath the apex and raised on a platform, is a soldier, taxidermied. He crouches in shooting position, stuffed white fingers curled around rifle trigger, one eye squints, the other eyeball stares straight ahead.

I am supposed to meet the Lead Taxidermist for orientation. She descends on the escalator behind the soldier. I see you're admiring our work, she says, looking over her glasses and placing a loose, gray dreadlock behind her ear. Yes, I say, it looks really lifelike. She says, honey, we are all *lifelike*. Huh? I say. I understand what you're saying, she says. But what I'm saying is, we only live in approximation to life, approaching what life *is*. Even dying is an attempt to approach life. That's how I perceive taxidermy. A representation of extant *and* extinct humans in that liminal space of approaching life.

Subject Interview #0250f

Of course, sugar, I'll answer any questions you want.

How did you come into this line of work?

Well, for twenty years I'd specialized in taxidermy for the other Great Apes: Chimpanzees, Gorillas, Bonobos, Orangutans. So the government contacted me when they dreamed up this little project of preserving Humans, the other Great Ape. They'd seen my work in various museums around the world. Most notably, the Zoologisk Museum at the University of Copenhagen in Denmark, where I taxied a Silverback Gorilla and his entire harem of four females along with two infants. Somehow they'd been poisoned in the Congo, the Democratic Republic. Gotta get the names right since you're publishing this. Anyway, lots of parallels can be drawn between performing taxidermy on the other Great Apes and Humans. Although bipedalism and glabrescence present their own particular sets of challenges, which we can discuss later.

I'm sorry, what does 'glabrescence' mean?

Oh don't be sorry. It's a pesky word anyway. It's the technical term for hairlessness. And do me a favor, please. Make sure you capitalize the names of the animals, they're proper names in my book.

[*Subject gives me a copy of her book*, Flesh of My Flesh: The Liminal Space of Taxidermy.]

Participation

The Lead Taxidermist unlocks a STAFF ONLY door and we walk down. There are four levels of the basement, she says, each is for a different part of the process. We descend three flights of concrete stairs, lit by emergency-exit green.

On the third level we walk into a room. Fluorescent lights hum a glow onto white-tiled walls, glossy white floors with black flecks, gun-gray cabinets. A 20×20 grid of stainless-steel tables with sinks at each end, and evenly spaced holes in the top surface. I circle my finger along one of the holes. To collect the drippings, she says.

The Lead Taxidermist zigzags from room to room. *Taxi*, means to arrange, she says, and of course, *derm*, means skin. She walks over to a stainless-steel cabinet with a glass door, digital red numbers: five degrees Celsius. These are ready to be mounted, she says, pointing with a pen. Flesh hangs, short-sleeved, rounded at the bottom like shirttails. Droopy black holes where eyes once were.

Right now, this is the only processing center, she says. We will begin shipping taxidermy to the five other museums being built around the country until they are fitted with their own processing centers. Lord knows when, but hopefully soon, we're so backlogged here.

This way, she says. At the end of the room is a large door, digital red again: zero degrees Celsius. Hanging next to the door is a clipboard, white paper rows and columns filled with text. This is our storage room for the bodies waiting to be taxied.

Inside the room, gush of cold vacuum-sealed air, stainless-steel ceilings revealed by successive motion-detected fluorescents. Stainless-steel trays stacked four high, four wide, separated by an aisle. Four more trays, another aisle, and I can't tell how far back they go. Each tray holds a stiff body, face up, covered by a white sheet.

Table	Name	Rank	Branch	Age	Date of Death	Cause Of Death	Place of Death	Cremate?
1		Captain	Army	30	9/29	Non-hostile – suicide[iii]	Baghdad	Y
2		Lance Corporal	Marines	19	10/14	Hostile Fire - IED attack	Baghdad	Y
3		Corporal	Marines	21	10/14	Hostile Fire – IED attack	Baghdad	Y
4		Specialist	Army	23	10/09	Hostile Fire – small arms fire	Baghdad	N
5		1st Lieutenant	Army	25	9/30	Hostile Fire – helicopter crash	Baghdad	Y
6		Sergeant	Army	28	9/28	Non-Hostile- suicide	Al Amarah	Y
7		Captain	Army	27	9/30	Hostile Fire – rocket attack	Wasit	Y
8		Specialist	Army	22	10/02	Non-Hostile- suicide	Wasit	N
9		Specialist	Army	21	10/05	Non-Hostile- suicide	Wasit	N
10		Specialist	Army N.G.	20	10/05	Hostile Fire – rocket attack	Wasit	Y
11		Private 1st Class	Army	19	10/31	Hostile Fire - grenade	Tikrit	Y
12		Commander	Army	49	9/03	Hostile Fire- suicide car bomb	Manama	Y
13		Corporal	Marines	25	9/01	Hostile Fire- suicide car bomb	Badrah	Y
14		Lance Corporal	Marines	26	9/01	Hostile Fire- suicide car bomb	Diyala	Y
15		Corporal	Army	22	8/29	Non-Hostile- friendly fire	Kandahar	N

Table	Name	Rank	Branch	Age	Date of Death	Cause Of Death	Place of Death	Cremate?
16	▰	Staff Sergeant	Army	23	8/29	Non-Hostile-friendly fire	Kandahar	Y
17	▰	Staff Sergeant	Army	24	8/29	Non-Hostile-friendly fire	Kandahar	Y
18	▰	Private 2nd Class	Army	19	8/29	Non-Hostile-friendly fire	Kandahar	Y
19	▰	Specialist	Army	25	8/29	Non-Hostile-friendly fire	Kandahar	Y
20	▰	Major General	Army	55	9/17	Non-Hostile-illness	Kabul	Y
21	▰	Petty Officer 2nd	Navy	23	10/02	Non-Hostile-vehicle accident	Bagram AFB	N
22	▰	Chief Petty Off.	Navy	35	10/02	Non-Hostile-vehicle accident	Bagram AFB	Y
23	▰	Airman 1st Class	Air Force	24	10/05	Hostile Fire-small arms fire	Bagram AFB	Y
24	▰	Tech. Sergeant	Air Force	30	10/06	Hostile Fire-small arms fire	Bagram AFB	Y
25	▰	Gunnery Sgt.	Marines	35	9/23	Hostile Fire-IED attack	Patika	Y
26	▰	Gunnery Sgt.	Marines	34	9/23	Hostile Fire-IED attack	Patika	Y
27	▰	Private	Marines	19	9/17	Non-Hostile-suicide	Baghdad	N
28	▰	Private	Marines	19	9/18	Non-Hostile-suicide	Baghdad	Y
29	▰	Private 1st Class	Army	20	9/19	Non-Hostile-suicide	Kabul	Y

We have to be careful not to let the temperature of this room fall below zero, she says, because ice will form in the body tissue and the skin will lose its wonderful elasticity. Hell, even at this temperature, we have to submerge the bodies in a boiler to thaw them. These bodies are assigned to the tables you saw in the previous room. The families can choose to receive an urn after we cremate the parts we don't use. The crematorium is on the fourth level.

The second level is where the skins are mounted. Rows of off-white muscled mannequins with hollow eye sockets pose: saluting, lying in sniper position, standing in shooting position, throwing grenades, crouching, running.

Next to each mannequin is a short gray cabinet with shallow drawers. She slides out the top drawer: egg-crate gray foam nests glass eyes. Pairs of brown, black, blue and green irises.

Next drawer: eyebrows and eyelashes, shades of brown, black and blond.

Next drawer: glove-like silicone hands with plastic fingernails.

I thought the hands were real skin when I saw that one guy in the lobby. Well that's the point, she says. But no, it's pretty difficult to remove the skin from hands, and then mount it. Plus, by using silicone, it's easier to position the hands around a trigger, tossing a grenade, saluting, or what have you. She slides the drawer back in place. The fatty parts of the face, like the lips and cheeks, are also filled with silicone. Look here.

We walk to another mounting station. See, Camilla here just filled in the lips with silicone. She looks up, but goes right back to stitching the skin down the back of the head and neck. The brown irises are in the sockets. The lips look naturally full. The rest of the skin is draped around the shoulders.

On the first level the mounted skins are fitted with uniforms. Boots are polished glossy, placed and laced up on the soldiers, sailors, airmen, marines. Their hands are fitted with rifles, handguns (real guns, but defunct). A Navy SEAL has his face painted black and green. A Marine is fitted with a pressed dress uniform, blue pants, black, gold-buttoned coat, left breast lined with medals, white belt, white-gloved hand saluting the black brim of his white cap.

Back out in the dull concrete stairwell, we walk down to the fourth level. Long room, a row of refrigerated body containers on each side, an arched brick crematory at the end. A man stands next to one of the containers tapping a clipboard with a pen. The Lead Taxidermist yells, Patrick, we have our volunteer. We walk closer, my head swivels between the bodies on each wall. Would you mind terribly if he watched the start of the process? Not at all, Patrick says, as long as he doesn't mind helping lift the cadaver onto the stretcher. Do you mind? No, I say.

Grasp the other end of the sheet, Patrick says. The cold yellow toenails scrape my wrist. Patrick grins. The flesh had been removed from the head and upper body, revealing gray muscle. But the flesh was still attached from forearms to fingertips. And from hips to toes. Flesh still attached to penis, a smooth line cut around the pubic hair. ■

Suicidal/homicidal: No
Client denied suicidal/homicidal ideation plan or intent.

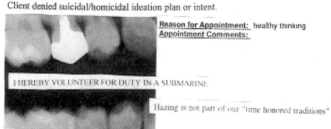

Reason for Appointment: healthy thinking
Appointment Comments:

I HEREBY VOLUNTEER FOR DUTY IN A SUBMARINE

Hazing is not part of our "time honored traditions"

Alleged Offender's Relationship To Victim: Intrafamilial/Spouse
Type of Maltreatment: Minor physical

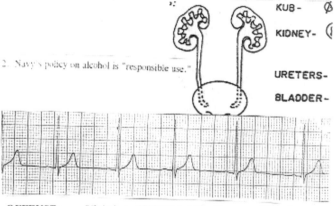

2. Navy's policy on alcohol is "responsible use."

KUB –

KIDNEY –

URETERS –

BLADDER –

OFFENSE: Violation of UCMJ Art.86, Absence without leave
Violation of UCMJ Art. 91, Insubordinate conduct
towards a noncommissioned officer
Violation of UCMJ Art 92 Failure to obey order or
regulation

PUNISHMENT AWARDED: Reduction to next inferior pay grade

1. Military life is fundamentally different from civilian life.

The military has its own laws, rules,

c. A member may be discharged by reason of parenthood

if it is determined the member,

because of parental responsibilities,

is unable to perform his or her duties satisfactorily or is

unavailable for worldwide assignment or deployment.

d. A member may be separated for violation of laws or regula
of members of the Armed Forces, for example,
homosexual or soliciting another to engage
homosexual bisexual, or words to that effec
individual of same sex. See reverse.

RESTRICTIONS ON ...SONAL CONDU... ...E ARMED FORCES

...s regarding sexual conduct
...ing to engage in a
...ati hat he or she is a
...tte ...ing to marry an
...for marrying
uch an act; fo
aging or atten

Mission To . . . 2016

THE ASTRONAUT

Christina Wood Martinez

Peter had difficulty sleeping when the astronauts began falling to Earth. We watched the television all night. The camera shifted between frames: the black speck, spotted miles above an Albany suburb, slowly descending as if caught in a bubble; magnified by ten, the astronaut in his white suit, suspended in the sky, his arms out, his palms turned back as if he were hugging the air behind him.

The television announcer's voice incanted: 'He has done what no man before him has done. What will he tell us of the frontier of the unknown?'

Peter sat at the edge of his recliner, barely resting his weight, and I thought he looked very much like our dog waiting at the front door, overeager to go on a walk.

A group of people gathered on the dairy farm where it was predicted the astronaut would land. They stood in groups of four, holding sheets taut between them. He drifted down slowly, like a feather. The breeze shifted him slightly west. The crowd cheered as he approached, but then grew quiet as the outline of his body, the red stripes on the legs of his suit, became clear. It was four nuns who caught him in a sheet and then set him carefully on the ground. They watched, and Peter and I watched, on the television, the astronaut lying on his back. The camera zoomed in. Everyone waited. Eventually, he stirred. He stood up, surveyed his surroundings, and walked through the parting crowd toward the road, his feet bouncing slightly off the ground.

N early every day a new astronaut touched down on Earth. The television showed them in their new places of work. They became bank tellers, factory machine operators, sign painters, postmen bouncing down country roads with their satchels of mail. They were celebrated, invited to dinners, pie bake-offs, parades. Auto dealerships and high school football teams changed their mascots to the man in a helmet and a white spacesuit. Astronaut-themed parties were all the rage and ladies' magazines printed recipes for lime-green space punch, asteroid crunch and moon melts. At socials, every girl lined up to dance with an astronaut. Peter and I were happy to see them integrating with society.

I sorted the laundry while we watched the press conference. Five representative astronauts, identical in their suits except for the middle astronaut who had a medal pinned to his chest, sat before a painting of the solar system with our flag mounted on the top pole of every planet.

The reporters flung questions: 'Is there life on other planets?' 'What does infinity look like?' 'Does space have a smell?' 'If we should happen to exhaust all of Earth's natural resources or destroy the planet, is there another planet, equally bountiful, to which we might relocate?'

But the astronauts gave no response.

'From a distance, was it possible, could you see, with grander perspective, Earth's place in the universe and the reason why we are all here?'

'Are the microphones on?' a reporter shouted. 'Can they even hear through their helmets?'

'Was it lonely up there?' another asked.

The astronaut with the medal nodded yes.

P eter dragged the television and its stand into the dining room and stationed it at one end of the table. We watched the coverage while we ate dinner.

'How was your day?' I asked.

'Shhhhhh,' Peter said.

'More chicken? Beans?' I wanted to needle him. 'Did Sandra call you? What about George, is he back on his feet again?'

Peter's eyes narrowed. I could see the light of the television in his pupils. He looked like a skinny old horse chewing hay. I served myself more green beans and began a mental list of the groceries I would need to pick up in town the next day.

When the news broke for commercials, he took a bite of chicken, leaned back and slipped his hand under the band of his pants, where I suspected there was the start of a hernia.

He saw me looking at his hand, and started up talking. 'That George Ziegler is the stupidest blunderbuss I know. Got his ankle twisted last week and today he buzzed the tip of his thumb off with a drill saw. Calls us blubbering some nonsense. Danger to himself. He should be put in a straitjacket.'

'Did he need stitches?' I considered clearing my plate, but let it be.

'Two.'

Peter had been a firefighter before his knees began to bother him. For the last ten years, he'd been working at the station answering the telephone, keeping the books, tidying up. Our town was small and sparsely spread through wooded hills. The firemen often served as medics for minor injuries and the fire truck as an ambulance when the doctor was tied up.

'Not so many then,' I said. I licked my finger and rubbed at a spot on the tablecloth. The conversation about whether George Ziegler, who had a metal plate in his head and perhaps shards of shrapnel beneath it, should really be living alone was not one worth picking up. The disagreement as old as stone, Peter's resolve to let the man be was no less obdurate.

I found myself talking. 'I did some weeding today – the garden is getting to be more dandelions than vegetables, but the roses are starting to bloom. I stewed fifteen pounds of tomatoes – they'll go into cans tonight if I have the energy for it. And when I was down in the basement I saw that one of the windows was cracked. A mouse came in, must have been through the hole, and got himself caught in the trap. I buried him in the rose bed, poor thing. I don't imagine a mouse would be comforted to know he's become nourishment for roses, but I suppose that's the circle of things.'

'Always something to fix,' Peter said. The news had come back on. He was back to chewing. I took our dishes into the kitchen and began to wash them. Our house was a patchwork of Peter's half-completed projects – the kitchen cupboards' missing doors, the unfinished screened-in porch, the table my father made, sanded but not stained. I set the dishes to dry on the rack next to the sink, and the water trickled between the tiles where the grout was scraped away. I dropped the dish towel on the floor to catch the drips.

In the morning I took the dog out for a walk. The sun was just beginning to light the sky and Peter was still asleep in his room downstairs. He snored and I was a light sleeper – we hadn't shared a bed in so many years I'd lost count.

The dog woke when I came downstairs. She was slow to get up – she was getting to be an old girl – but she wagged her tail and did the mincing dance she always did while I fetched her leash. I held her face in my hands and looked into her eyes – her wild excitement so close to a look of terror, or perhaps it was unconditional love.

We set out. The grass was wet and bowed with dew, the trees were fringed with bright new spring leaves, and we saw a mother duck with six ducklings waddling through the woods toward the stream. We stopped in the meadow and I released the dog from her leash and sat down on a stump – our usual routine. She ran off and I rested with my thoughts.

As it often did, my mother's face came to me – not as I had last seen it when she was sick and dying in our guest bedroom, the treatment having run its course, but from a photograph of her as a young woman. My sister and I were on her lap, her arms around us, her teeth parted, smiling, as though she had just taken in a great breath of summer air. I don't remember the photo being taken – I was so small, and Iris was only an infant. Iris – I received a letter from her a few days before. She was a grandmother again – she had her children young and was now rich with grandchildren. She included a Polaroid of the new baby, a girl.

I thought about Peter. Once, when we were newly married, he found beetles tinier than poppy seeds crawling through the bread of the sandwich he had eaten half of. His face grew red, and he kept eating the sandwich until it was finished.

I laughed a little. I wasn't always sure why I thought the things I thought.

I whistled, but the dog didn't hear me. I hollered her name. After a moment, she came running back, all muddied, smiling her dog's smile. 'Good girl,' I said. When we returned home, I would make bacon for her, and Peter would come into the kitchen pouting, asking where his was.

At the house, I kicked the mud off my shoes. Peter came running up to me in his overalls, out of breath.

'Come here! Come here!' He was waving his arms. I sighed and followed.

He had been mowing the field of wild grass behind the house. It hadn't been tended to in quite a long time – it was tall and had gone to seed – and hidden in it was the astronaut. He lay unmoving in his suit, flat on his back.

'Should we call the fire department?' I asked.

Peter touched him with the toe of his shoe. After a moment, the astronaut stirred. We watched him rise to his feet. He looked around, at our house, at the copse of elm trees that bordered our yard, and then at us. He was tall. His helmet peaked nearly a foot above our heads.

'Sir, would you like to come inside?' Peter asked.

The astronaut looked at the house and began walking toward it.

His boots bounced over the freshly cut grass.

I made tea while the astronaut sat at our kitchen table and gazed out the window. I rinsed some grapes and set them out. The dog wove in and out of the kitchen, taking a glance, then turning about-face for the living room, tail between her legs.

'Some trip!' Peter said. 'Must have been quite a view. How was the ride down? Any turbulence?'

I placed a teacup before the astronaut – our nice china – but he didn't take it.

Peter went on talking. 'You picked a good day to land. Decent weather out, low wind. Another astronaut got caught in a storm over Chesapeake – blown right out over the Atlantic. Lucky thing a longliner spotted him and scooped him up. Say, what'd you see up there? Any moon men?'

The astronaut's black visor stared out the window.

Peter told the astronaut about all the coverage on the news. One astronaut was made employee of the month at an auto plant. Another found a lost dog but refused the reward. One became a policeman and stopped a bank robbery. The bank was going to commission a statue of him.

'We'll find work that will suit you, too,' Peter said. 'Of course, ours is a small community. There aren't so many jobs that a man can take his pick, but we can surely put a pair of able hands to work. What skills do you have?'

The astronaut turned his head toward the dog who whimpered, but also, full of hope, wagged her tail.

Peter grew quiet. The astronaut's suit drifted woozily back and forth in his chair.

'You must be tired,' I said. The astronaut turned his helmet to face me. 'Come, why don't you rest for a bit.'

He rose, and I showed him to Peter's room, also the guest room, where he lay down atop the coverlet. I closed the door quietly and we didn't hear him stir for the rest of the day.

That night, Peter and I whispered in bed.

'I'll call Dr Shiner in the morning,' I said. 'He's been a long time up there. He may need medical attention.'

'He's an astronaut,' Peter said. 'He'll ask for help if he needs it.'

'But regardless, we should let someone know he's here.'

'Certainly,' Peter said. 'The guys at the station won't be able to stand it – an astronaut in my own backyard!'

Peter rolled over to face me and I thought for a moment that he might kiss me, but he finished adjusting his pajama pants and rolled away to lie on his back. He snored all night, and I drifted in and out of sleep, dreaming of an astronaut floating through the rings of Saturn.

In the morning, the astronaut could not be found. I saw that all the dishes I had washed the night before were put away. The bed in the guest room was made. The dog was asleep on the kitchen floor with her toy beside her – it seemed she had already been let out to relieve herself. Peter finally spotted him outside in the backyard, sun gleaming on his white suit. He had just finished mowing the lawn.

Peter said to me, putting his hands in his overall pockets, 'Maybe he can give us a hand around here for a little while.'

For a time, the astronaut was always busy. He dusted and mopped. He mulched and aerated the soil in our garden, now more vegetable than dandelion. He cleaned the windows, fixed my wind chime, repainted the front door a lovely pale blue. Peter called in sick. 'Come on, champ,' he said. Together they finished the kitchen cupboard doors, stained the table, re-grouted the countertops, patched the leaky roof and hammered on new shingles.

The astronaut was a great cook, though he didn't like to prepare or eat meat. He made bread from scratch and prepared the vegetable sides while I did the main. Each night we sat down to dinner, the three of us – Peter with the astronaut's pork chop or chicken thigh on his plate – and watched the television, eating from trays in the living room.

Peter didn't like to watch the news anymore. He changed the

channel if something about the astronauts came on. Instead, we watched evening programming, *Bonanza* and *I Dream of Jeannie*.

Aside from when my mother was ill, Peter and I had never shared our home with anyone else and we didn't have much family to speak of. My father was killed in the first war. I had memories, but Peter, whose father enlisted early, didn't. Peter's mother died of a stroke two months after we married. My sister married and moved away as soon as she turned eighteen. And we didn't know if it was Peter or me, though I had always assumed it was me. Either way, we never had children.

It was nice having company in the house, and the astronaut's countenance now seemed somehow cheerful. Each evening, he and Peter tossed a baseball back and forth in the yard. Peter liked to entertain him with stories of his time in the war and the astronaut's helmet followed Peter around the living room as he pantomimed tossing a grenade, crawling on his hands and knees behind the recliner to demonstrate life in the trenches.

I saw the astronaut's helmet bob sometimes, while we watched *The Tonight Show*, as if he were laughing. He liked to sit at the end of the couch, so the dog could jump up between us and rest her chin on his leg. He patted her head with his glove, and she looked up at him with that wild look in her eyes.

'June Daltry called today to invite us over for a dinner party,' I whispered to Peter while we lay in bed. 'I know you wouldn't want to go, but I thought maybe I could bring the astronaut instead. Wouldn't that be a conversation starter?'

Peter pursed his lips and kept his eyes on his newspaper.

'And, really, shouldn't we bring him to the elementary school? The children would just be delighted. I could call the principal tomorrow. And maybe there are other astronauts in the area – over in Dewsbury or Fulton. He should meet others like him. We've really kept him cooped up here.'

Peter turned away from me and pulled the covers up to his chin. 'Peter?'

I heard him groan. 'He doesn't want to listen to Roger's asinine jokes or eat June's mushy food. She is a silly woman who laughs like a goat. And who would want a bunch of kids climbing all over him like a damned jungle gym? No sense of respect. He's just not interested in any of those things.'

I sat next to the astronaut on the sofa, mending a sock. He held the yarn for me, turning the ball when I needed more slack. He and Peter had run out of projects, and the house was as tidy as could be.

'Would you like to learn how to sew?' I asked.

The astronaut nodded.

I fetched my sewing box. All the astronaut's help around the house freed me up to start a rag quilt to send to my sister's new granddaughter.

'First you thread the needle, like this,' I said. I wet it between my lips and held it up so he could see. 'You try.'

His gloves were too thick and he couldn't manage the needle.

I patted his glove. 'You just keep me company.'

A song my mother used to sing came to mind – when I was a child, we were always singing. There were times we spent a whole evening just singing with the lights off to save electricity, seated on the rug in front of the fireplace on a snowy night. I sang a few of those old songs for the astronaut. After a while, he seemed to doze. His helmet slumped, hovering above my shoulder. He stayed like that, but I wouldn't have minded at all, it would have been nice, really, if he had rested his head on me.

That night I had a dream about the astronaut. We were walking through the dense woods, and I could hear him breathing heavily through his helmet. The dog was beside us, sniffing along the trail, and then she was gone. The astronaut walked on – he seemed to know where we were going – and after some time we came upon a pool fed by a stream. There were silver fish darting along the surface, waiting for insects to fall in.

The astronaut pointed to a spot along the bank. I lay on the ground there and he stood beside me, looking down. I could see myself in his visor, my hair fanned all around. I could feel water seeping into the heels of my shoes. He kneeled then and put one hand on his wrist. He twisted his glove and pulled it off. There were black hairs on the back of his hand and his knuckles. He rested his hand on my thigh, then slid his fingers up and touched me between my legs.

I was awake then – the room was dark still, it was the middle of the night and Peter snored beside me. I didn't stir. I closed my eyes and tried to return to the dream, urging it onward.

I woke early and made him a special breakfast: eggs over-medium and freshly squeezed orange juice and pancakes with bananas and cocoa in the batter.

When he came into the kitchen, I shouted, 'Surprise! A special breakfast, just for you.'

I sang a verse of 'For He's a Jolly Good Fellow' and sat down – I found I was flushed, out of breath. I had styled my hair a new way. I felt silly. He took a seat at the table, looked down at his plate – at the smiling face I had drawn with chocolate syrup on his pancake. I ran my fingers through my hair to undo the curls.

There were reports of astronauts who had trouble integrating. One got up from his post quality-checking metal washers and entirely disappeared. One made a scene at a restaurant, refusing to pay his check and knocking over the restaurant's sidewalk sign as he fled in his car. One had beaten his neighbor, for no known reason. The man lay unconscious in a hospital bed.

'I thought he was a wonderful neighbor,' the man's wife said in an interview – she stood wide-eyed in slippers outside her front door. 'He helped Richard clear the storm drains.'

A politician made speeches saying we ought to quarantine them, test them, make sure they were of sound mind and ideology and fit to live among us. That we ought to discover, once and for all and by any means necessary, what exactly they had come to know of the great mysteries that lay beyond our atmosphere.

'Our children call them heroes,' the politician said, 'and yet they do not tell us if there are dangers that await us in what lies beyond. Our towns welcome them, and yet we do not know that they are not traitors, spies, living among us. It is all of mankind's right to know what they know, what they have seen, and yet they refuse to tell us. Why could this be except that they are no friends of ours and they intend to do us harm?'

I didn't like the astronaut seeing these sorts of things. I watched a bit of the news while he was out walking the dog, and then I kept the set off while we ate our breakfast.

One evening, Peter came home from work later than usual. The astronaut and I were eating dinner, a vegetarian quiche, off TV trays, watching a program about an astronaut-turned-detective who solved particularly mysterious crimes. Peter came in and switched the television off. He stood in front of the set with his hands on his hips.

'Tomorrow, we're going pheasant hunting!' he declared.

He took one of our china plates – a collectible – painted with the image of a pheasant, and showed it to the astronaut. The astronaut dusted the plate and returned it carefully to its spot in the curio cabinet while Peter, who hadn't been hunting in at least ten years, spent the evening cleaning his rifle and recounting memories of his greatest shots. The astronaut seemed withdrawn, but Peter took no notice. He made ham sandwiches and filled a flask with Scotch.

'Good luck,' I said from under the covers the next morning as Peter dressed without turning on the light.

'Luck has nothing to do with it,' Peter said.

They didn't return until sunset. Peter came indoors singing, with four pheasants strung over his shoulder.

'Quite the haul! Did you shoot any?' I asked the astronaut. He was turned away, shoulders slumped, looking in the sink for dishes to wash.

'No,' Peter responded for him, avoiding my eye. 'I told him pheasants are ground birds, but the goof kept looking up at the sky.'

He glanced at the astronaut and whispered to me, 'I think it's that helmet. Makes it hard for him to see.'

Feathers were dropping all over the kitchen floor. The astronaut found the broom and swept them up.

The next day, he slept through most of the morning. The guest-room door remained closed. We didn't hear him stirring inside.

'Maybe he's sick,' I whispered to Peter. 'I'll call Dr Shiner.'

'He's fine,' Peter said. He picked up the keys to his truck. 'Nothing refreshes a man like working with his hands.'

At lunchtime, I knocked quietly on the astronaut's door. It was silent inside. I opened it and saw him lying in bed, flat on his back atop the covers, his arms at his sides. I carried in a bowl of tomato soup and some crackers. I set a vase with the last of the autumn roses, pale peach and sweet-smelling, on his nightstand.

There was slight movement beneath his spacesuit. It was his chest, moving up and down. I could see him breathing. Who's in there? I wondered.

I patted his glove to see if he would wake. I touched his wrist, where his glove connected to the arm of his suit. I twisted it, thinking of his hand, such large hands, perfectly formed, soft, with black hair on the knuckles.

Peter let the back door slam shut. He came to the guest-room door, carrying a hammer. I stood up and put my finger to my lip. 'Shhhhh!' I said. 'He's sleeping.' I left the room and closed the door.

'But I've got a new project for us,' he said.

'Let him rest,' I told him.

Peter's shoulders slumped. 'Looks like rain anyway.'

The astronaut kept to his room the following day. It drizzled outside. But the next morning, I woke late to sounds of shoveling and hammering, and he and Peter were already laying the foundations for a new shed. I watched them work from the kitchen window. It looked as though the old shed, already big enough, would be dwarfed by the new one. I would have to listen to their hammering for a month.

I'd had another dream about him the night before. We were walking someplace strange where the trees were smooth, tall columns with green orbs in the place of leaves. The air was still and the sun hung low and red in the sky. We walked for quite some time – he held my hand and led me on and I felt excited, giddy, though I didn't know where we were going. After a while, he stopped and turned to me. The red sun reflected in his visor. He touched his helmet. He began to lift it off, and I saw his clefted chin, his lips.

Now, outside, Peter was gesturing wildly, telling a story while the astronaut used the saw. He had bought the astronaut a tool belt identical to his.

For Peter's birthday, the astronaut made scalloped potatoes and creamed spinach and biscuits and baked a yellow layer cake with chocolate frosting. I fried the steaks in lard.

When Peter came home from work he kissed me on the cheek. I could hardly hide my surprise.

'Happy birthday, dear,' I said.

He opened his gifts – a new wool pullover from me and a birdhouse from the astronaut. He'd made and painted it himself. While we ate, I asked Peter if the firemen had celebrated his birthday at work.

'I don't like to go around tooting my own horn,' Peter said. 'The phone only rang once, and that's a good enough gift for me.'

'Not George, I hope?'

'No, Mrs Dean spotted an opossum walking down her driveway in the middle of the day, so she called us over to take a look. Found it by the creek bed, running back and forth, foaming at the mouth, definitely rabid. Mike grabbed it by the tail and gave it a good whack on the head and then we saw a bunch of little ones in the weeds nearby – they must have been her babies, following her around. I caught those and put them in a sack. Wasn't much to do but drown them. They looked okay, but they were probably too small to make it on their own.'

'What a shame,' I said.

I sang happy birthday and we cut the cake, but the astronaut didn't touch his. Peter was in the middle of a long story when the astronaut slowly rose from his chair and left the room.

'What's the matter with him now?' Peter asked.

After cleaning up, I looked for the astronaut and found him standing in the basement, looking out the window that was no bigger than a breadbox.

'Are you okay?' I asked. I put my hand on his shoulder.

Peter appeared at the top of the stairs. 'Sulking again, eh?' he asked.

The astronaut began to turn around.

'Oh come on now! What's your reason to sulk? You came to us as a stranger and we took you in. I give you free room and board and haven't asked a thing in return. You don't even know the talk that's going on out there. Astronauts deserting, getting violent, won't tell us a damn thing about all the time they spent up there floating around – people are shaken up!'

'Peter,' I said.

'No!' He was shouting now. 'You can't bite the hand that feeds you – it just isn't civil!'

He slammed the basement door, but it banged out of the jamb and swung open again. The floorboards creaked above our heads.

That night, I thought about going to him, sitting at the edge of his bed, apologizing on Peter's behalf. I imagined he would rest his head on my shoulder and I would sing to comfort him. I imagined he would put his arms around my waist and pull my body to his.

I tiptoed downstairs – I thought I ought at least check to make sure he was asleep.

The guest room was empty and I could hear the television in the living room. I thought Peter must have left the set on when he came to bed, but there was the astronaut, sitting in Peter's recliner, with all the lights off, watching the news. The anchor was reporting on the vote that Congress was soon to cast on the astronaut issue.

The astronaut was looking at me and I could see myself in his visor – there was the blue light of the television and then me, barefoot and brassiereless in my pink nightgown, curlers in my hair, a pink moon at orbit in space. I wondered what he could have thought of me.

The astronaut nodded. I took it as a 'goodnight' and went back upstairs and took my place next to Peter, who was mumbling in his sleep.

In the morning, he was gone. Peter looked all over the house, the yard, the woods.

'What if he's lost?' he said, pacing in the kitchen. He was nearly shouting. 'What if someone took him?'

Peter spent the day hammering, frantically working on the shed. Then, as night encroached, I watched him, from the kitchen window, kick the frame of it until it fell to the ground, splintered in pieces. I turned away from the window and began to put away the dishes that the astronaut had washed the day before.

Peter and I watched, on the television, the shuttle launch. A team of astronauts, former postmen and substitute teachers and telephone repairmen, returning to space, back to where they came from. We saw the footage of them walking up the gangway into the shuttle, one by one, dozens of them, their white suits and helmets bobbing up and down. They wanted to go back. They saluted as they entered the shuttle.

Peter crouched close to the television and looked carefully at each

one, but we had no way of knowing if he was there, or which he was
– which one of them was our astronaut.

'I'm at a loss,' Peter said.

There was a countdown and then the shuttle's contrail bisected
the sky.

P eter moved back into the guest room without a word. I lay in bed
and imagined that the astronaut, the night before he left, had
come into my room and woken me with his hand on my chest, taking
mine in his glove. I rose, I went with him to the yard where the moon
was low and yellow. We began to float up, he and I, leaving the Earth
behind, toward that large and blinking sheet of darkness. It wasn't
a dream. I couldn't sleep that night.

I thought of Peter, too: snoring in the astronaut's room, or perhaps
also awake, looking up at the ceiling, his eye turned not to where I was
lying in our bedroom right above him, but beyond, thinking too of
nebulas and stars, of the place where the astronaut had gone. It was
his fault. I hoped he knew. ■

THE LAST CHILDREN
OF TOKYO

Yoko Tawada

TRANSLATED FROM THE JAPANESE BY MARGARET MITSUTANI

The results of children's 'monthly look-overs' were copied by hand, then delivered to the Central Division of the New Japan Medical Research Center by a foot messenger. A popular manga entitled *A Message from the Sea Breeze*, about a foot messenger with the legs of a Japanese antelope and a map of every town in the country in his head, inspired lots of children to dream of becoming foot messengers when they grew up, though the general deterioration in physical strength among the young would make that impossible for most. In the near future, young people would probably all work in offices while physical labor was left to the elderly.

All original data concerning children's health was recorded by hand, with each doctor hiding his patients' data in a place of his own choosing. There were cartoons in the newspaper showing doctors squirreling documents away in dog houses, or at the bottom of huge cauldrons. Though Yoshiro laughed when he saw them, it later occurred to him that this might be reality rather than satire.

Because the data that each clinic delivered to the Medical Research Center were handwritten copies of handwritten originals, any attempt at erasing or tampering with large amounts of data would take an awfully long time. In this sense, the current system was safer than the security systems invented by even the best computer programmers in earlier times.

Now that the adjective 'healthy' didn't really fit any child, pediatricians were not only working longer hours, but also had to face the parents' anger and sadness alone, as well as feeling pressure from unknown sources whenever they tried to explain the situation to newspapers or other public media. Many suffered from insomnia or were driven to suicide, until finally the surviving pediatricians formed a labor union, boldly announcing a reduction in their working hours, refusing to submit reports demanded by insurance companies and cutting all ties with major pharmaceutical firms.

Mumei liked his pediatrician, so he never minded going for his monthly look-over. Visits to the dentist were as exciting to him as a school excursion – only Yoshiro found them depressing. Mumei loved sitting high up in the chair, talking to the dentist. On a recent visit, the dentist had said, 'You mustn't force milk on children who hate the smell. And even if they like it, you shouldn't give them too much.'

'Yes, I've heard that,' said Yoshiro, while the dentist peered down at Mumei and asked gravely, 'Do you like milk?'

Without skipping a beat Mumei replied, 'I like worms better.' Unable to see the line that connected milk to worms, in his confusion Yoshiro let his eyes wander outside the window, yet the dentist didn't seem the least bit perturbed. 'I see,' he said, 'so that means you're a baby bird rather than a calf. While calves drink their mother's milk, baby birds eat the worms their parents bring them. But worms live in the earth, so when the earth is contaminated, the contamination gets concentrated in the worms. That's why birds don't eat many worms these days. Which explains why there are so many worms now that it's easy to catch one. After it rains, you see lots of them squirming around in the middle of the road. You'd better not eat those leftover worms, though. It's better to stick to bugs you catch flying through the air.'

He sounded so matter-of-fact he might have been explaining how teeth should be brushed. Did knowing Yoshiro was a writer make him want to compete, to send his words flying off somewhere no writer would think to go? Or had Mumei and the dentist already progressed to some future dimension, leaving him far behind?

Many dentists like to show off their speaking skills, probably because the more they talk the longer their beautiful teeth are on display. This dentist was about to celebrate his 105th birthday, yet his jaw was still firm, his mouth lined with big, square teeth, gleaming white. Yoshiro was secretly thinking how he'd like to steal those fine teeth to give to his great-grandson when the dentist opened his mouth and started talking again.

'According to one theory, it's best to get your calcium from the bones of fish and animals. But they have to be from before the earth became irreversibly contaminated. So some people say we should dig way, way down underground to find dinosaur bones. In Hokkaido there are already shops that sell powder from ground Naumann's Elephant bones they've dug up there.'

By some strange coincidence the very next day, when he was passing the elementary school, Yoshiro happened to see a poster announcing a lecture on the Naumann's Elephant, to be given by a university professor of paleontology at the Cultural Park, and because lectures were a hobby of his, as soon as he got home he wrote 'Naumann's Elephant' on the wall calendar. Mumei stopped in his tracks every time he passed the calendar, blinking furiously, his eyes glued to the words 'Naumann's Elephant'. To Mumei, the words themselves were an animal that would start moving if only he stared at it long enough.

To break the spell that had nailed Mumei to the floor in front of the calendar, Yoshiro said, 'Naumann's Elephant is a kind of creature that lived some 300,000 years ago. Some professor's going to come give a talk about it. Why don't we go hear him?' His face lit up with joy, Mumei thrust both arms above his head, shouting, 'Paradise!' as he jumped up in the air. Though surprised at the time, Yoshiro later forgot all about Mumei's amazing leap.

It wasn't just Naumann's Elephant that cast a spell on Mumei.

When he heard or saw the word heron, for instance, or sea turtle, he became obsessed, unable to take his eyes off the name from which he believed a living creature might emerge.

Encountering a real animal – not just its name – would have set Mumei's heart on fire, but wild animals had not been seen in Japan for many years. As a student, Yoshiro had traveled to Kyoto through the mountains along the Nakasendo Trail with a German girl from a town called Mettmann. He had been shocked to hear her say, 'The only wild animals in Japan are spiders and crows.' Now that the country was closed to the outside world, no more visitors came from afar to wake people up with jabs like this. Whenever he thought about animals, Yoshiro remembered the German girl. Her name was Hildegard. She and Yoshiro were the same age. Sometimes he still heard her voice saying, 'Hello, Yo-shi-ro?' Even now, when there were no telephones, he would hear an electronic buzz in the air followed by 'Hello' repeated several times, then, 'Yo-shi-ro?' her voice, the way it rose, still reverberating in his ears. After 'Yo' she would take a breath, then sweep upward on 'shi', turning up the volume before the final 'ro', which cut the name short yet nevertheless sounded like a kind gesture, a welcoming hand stretched out.

Then the conversation would begin, in broken English. Yoshiro would ask a series of simple questions, like 'What did you eat today?' or 'Where do you buy vegetables?' or 'Do little kids in Germany like to play outside?' He was dying to know if the environment in Germany was unchanged, or becoming more contaminated like Japan, and whether her grandchildren and great-grandchildren were healthy. Hildegard would reply, 'I'm boiling the green beans I grew in my garden along with some herbs,' and at that moment, Yoshiro would be breathing in the steam rising from her saucepan, yet soon the voice on the other end of his imaginary telephone would grow too faint to hear, leaving him unable to tell whether he had actually heard her voice or just imagined it. Real or not, when he closed his eyes he could see this scene: Hildegard's great-grandchildren running around in the garden, jumping over a pond, standing on tiptoe to pluck apples from a tree, not even bothering to wash them before biting into the sour, worm-eaten fruit with their strong, white teeth. The apple eaten, they'd be wondering whether to pick wild flowers in the fields or go to the creek to watch the fish.

Yoshiro wanted to visit Hildegard in Germany, just once, but the routes from Japan to all foreign countries had been cut off. Perhaps that was why he no longer felt the roundness of the earth beneath his feet. The round earth he could travel across existed only in his head. There was nothing to do but follow that curve in his mind to the other side of the world.

Yoshiro imagined himself packing a small suitcase with clothes and toiletries, then taking the train and bus to Narita Airport. It had been years since he had been to Shinjuku – what was it like now? Billboards, far too gaudy to be overlooking ruins; traffic lights changing regularly from red to green on streets without a single car; automatic doors opening and closing for nonexistent employees, reacting, perhaps, to big branches on the trees that lined the streets, bending downwards in the wind. In banquet halls, the smell of cigarettes smoked long ago froze in the silver silence; at table after table in the pubs on each floor of multi-tenant buildings customers called absence caroused, drinking and eating their fill for a flat fee; with no one to borrow money, the interest demanded by loan sharks rusted in its tracks; without buyers, mounds of bargain underwear grew damp and fetid; mold formed on handbags displayed in show windows now flooded with rainwater, while rats took leisurely naps inside high-heeled shoes. From cracks in the asphalt, stalks of shepherd's purse grew straight up, two meters high. Now that human beings had disappeared from this urban center, the cherry trees that had once stood demurely beside sidewalks, slender as brooms, had grown thicker around the trunk, their branches spreading boldly out in all four directions, their luxuriant green Afros swaying gently back and forth in the breeze.

Yoshiro imagined himself at Shinjuku Station, boarding a deserted Narita Express for the airport. In fact, no one was riding the express,

the train whose foreign name had once projected the very image
of speed, or drinking espresso either. At the airport terminal there
was no one at the checkpoint, so no need to show his passport. The
terminal sign, written in Chinese characters, had been taken down
long ago, and was now propped up against a wall. Climbing the
creaky steps of the motionless escalator, he found all the check-in
counters abandoned, a huge spiderweb covering each one like an
umbrella. Looking more closely, he saw that there was a spider about
the size of the palm of his hand in each one, calmly waiting for prey.
There were colorful stripes on one spider's back; black at the top, red,
then yellow. Germany was his destination – that must explain it, he
thought. He took a cautious look at the counter next door and saw
that its spider had red, white and blue stripes. There were smaller red
spiders here and there in the web too, with white stars on their backs.

Yoshiro didn't know why he was able to picture the airport so
clearly. With no effort on his part, these images just came to him,
begging to be written into a novel. But it would be dangerous to write
about an airport nobody went to anymore. What if the government
was keeping it off limits to the public on purpose, because state
secrets were hidden there? Sneaking into a forbidden place to dig up
forbidden knowledge didn't interest him at all. But even if what he
published as fiction was only a description of what he had imagined,
if it happened to correspond too closely to what the airport was really
like he might be arrested for leaking state secrets. Proving in a court of
law that it had come from his imagination might be awfully difficult.
And would they even give him a trial? Not that he found the idea of
going to prison particularly frightening, but wondering how Mumei
would survive without him worried him so much that he couldn't
bring himself to take too many risks.

THE LAST CHILDREN OF TOKYO

How many years had it been since the absence of animals other than rental dogs and dead cats had ceased to bother him? Though he had heard something about a 'rabbit union' formed by people who secretly kept rabbits, since he didn't know anyone who belonged, he couldn't even show Mumei a living rabbit.

'Mumei, are you going to be a zoologist?' he would ask as he watched Mumei totally absorbed in drawing a zebra, copying the picture from his *Illustrated Guide to Animals*. In the old man's dreams, Mumei not only became a professor of zoology, but traveled the world, observing wild animals, writing essays about his travels that would make his name as a writer as well. This dream always softened his face with a smile that never took long to freeze into a frown. ∎

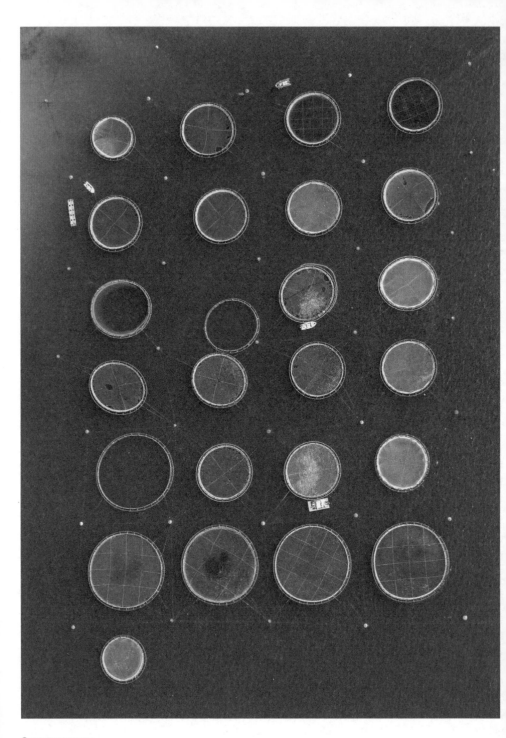

Fish Farms 003, 2017
from the *Fish Farms* series

ISSUE

Cormac James

I want you to close your eyes. I want you to relax, let go. I want you to let your mind see as vividly as possible the images my words conjure up. And above all, no matter what I say, I want you to trust me. When I say *trust me*, what I mean is, *feel safe*. Because I know exactly where we're going, every step of the way. We're going there together, you and me. Not for one moment will you be left alone. Never again. Never again that feeling of being forgotten, unimportant, left behind. How can I be so sure? That's easy. Because even with your eyes closed, as long as you can hear my voice you'll know exactly where I am.

Now. What I want you to imagine first is a large circular structure with no roof. Maybe the image that comes to mind is something like a corral or a bullring, but that's too big. Maybe you think of a circus ring instead, which is better, but this thing is much deeper than that. It has much higher walls. Like a Wall of Death, you wonder? Think Wall of Death if that helps. But filled with water, almost to the brim, and emitting a dull industrial hum. Hear it, as best you can. See it from above. Like you're hovering above it, looking down, the way they say you hover above your own body in a hospital bed when you're just about to die. Like in the movies, you think? That's good. That's exactly what I mean. We're on the same wavelength now.

From that height, you can see the water inside this thing swirling, not unlike water going down a plughole. Slightly dipped in the centre and swollen at the circumference. But looking closer you see that this swirling is not the only movement in the giant tub. Wedded to it is something deeper or darker, as though an invisible hand were twirling a giant length of seaweed round and round, entraining the rotation of the water itself. In fact, looking closer again, you notice not one but dozens of dark ribbons wheeling, from the hollow bullseye right out to the rim. More, you see that each circle is not a continuous thick thread but many segments – it's all coming into focus now, as in a particularly vivid dream – it's a huge tank filled with water, and full of huge fish, all the same colour, shape and size. *The same* does not mean similar. It does not mean merely of common species. These fish are all replicas, down to the last detail. Do you understand? In colour, they are a dull tin underneath and up the sides, and on top a dull brown, like trout. No green or blue. None of the glitz or glamour of tropical fish. Round and round they go, all at precisely the same pace, making it impossible to tell if it's the current carrying them along, like flotsam, or if it's their own effort that produces the unending clockwise wash. Maybe the image reminds you of those old cowboy movies you watched on Saturday mornings as a kid, with the Indians (as you called them then) circling the wagons endlessly, getting picked off one by one, and still they kept circling, circling, which never made any sense to you, did it? I've put that image in your mind and now I want you to forget it, if you can. That's hard, I know. But I want you to focus on my words as you hear them, in strict sequence, and one after the other to enjoy the concrete images they create in your mind. Now, for instance, I want you to look up and see dozens and dozens of identical tubs laid out in perfectly spaced rows in every direction, almost as far as the eye can see. It's some kind of laboratory fish farm on a scale beyond anything you've ever imagined. Looking into the distance, you see that what you'd taken for fairly shallow tubs resemble, in fact, roofless silos, of the kind used in the food and feed and petrochemical industries. The sides are corrugated-metal sheets, giving them a vintage look, and several storeys high, meaning each must contain tens of thousands of circling fish. Looking directly down again, you see no bottom to the well, if you can think of it as a kind of well, the light can't penetrate so much living flesh, it's so tightly packed, think crowd surge, think pilgrim crush, wheeling about the Kaaba, moving as every human crush moves, with what seems a commanding biological drive. Each individual is man-sized, with certain features – the pointed tail fins, the pointed head – not altogether unlike those of a shark. It also has a ridge running the length of its back that would not be out of place on a dinosaur. They are sturgeon.

Now I want you to imagine a change of scenery, but with the same cast. Same family, new house, if you will. I want you to imagine those same man-sized fish, in their tens of thousands, still turning those same circles, but doing so in the middle of the Atlantic. I don't mean dispersed. Exactly the opposite. They're still gathered in a tall, tightly packed column that goes from the surface down into the depths. Still contained, no longer within a sheet-metal silo, but within a cage more or less the same shape and size. This cage is moored to massive apple-green buoys, which are in turn anchored to the sea floor, a few miles off the coast of Tenerife. In the seawater, the circling fish are no less stunning than before, they haven't changed, and no surprise there, they've evolved so little in a hundred million years, *living fossils* they've been called, yet here they're treated like battery hens, just as the open sea under their cages is treated as an open sewer. I mean the dead zones on the seabed under the endless rain of antibiotics, uneaten feed, dead flesh, shit, I'm ranting now, I know, I like to rant, it calms me, it's a way of draining off some of this rage I have, there's so much of it, what a waste. I blame the cages, not the fish. Sea trout, salmon, shrimp, it doesn't matter, they're all as bad and they're spreading, even to the world's most remote havens, like the seaborne raiders of old – Greek, Trojan, Viking, take your pick – bringing death and destruction wherever they go, from the jewelled waters of the Aegean to Sicily, to Gozo, north to every Irish estuary, as far off as the Outer Hebrides, to the Norwegian fjords. Off the Azores there are cages stuffed with triggerfish, tuna, amberjack. There are gilt-head sea bream off Madeira. Red porgy and yellowtail off Lanzarote. And here, in Tenerife, in their cages, is where our giant sturgeon are to be found. I could go on, but I won't. These remote volcanic islands are the perfect place to stop.

Flush with the surface of the Atlantic, a metal walkway rounds the top of each sea cage, outside a handrail, like the paddock at a racetrack. The cages themselves are not visible. That is the ocean's great advantage. Almost everything unpleasant happens out of sight.

If I had more time, I'd love to recite a list of my favourite words, to see their effect on you. I call them crimes. The aquaculture industry calls them something else. *Benthic. Infestation. Faecal. Algal. Bloom.* The jargon has a feudal music, to my ears, and simply saying those words aloud has a calming effect I can't quite explain, just as my rants calm me when I'm in a rage. Think of me as an anxious child, if that helps. Think of this as a story I want to hear over and over again, especially the scary parts. I'm someone who's always liked picking at threads, stickers, scabs. There's something in loosening a knot, too, I've always found hard to resist. If that rope is bound to something at sea, better still. For once, I say, let something or someone else take the reins. Let tide or current tow the cages away, into an orbit from which they'll never escape. It is abandon, in every sense of the word, like leaving a comatose drunk on a fairground carousel.

I say *loose, release, abandon*, but even as I unmoor the sturgeons' sea cages I know well where they're bound. They will sail the same current that drew Columbus down from Cadiz to the Canaries, where we are now, and onward, west, and then north, across the calms of Cancer, then east, past the Azores, back to the starting point to begin again, and what's particularly pleasing, you must agree, is to imagine those magnificent fish spinning endlessly as they go, even as each cage itself turns a vast, slow circle, the same way our planet spins on its axis as it makes its year-long orbit of the sun. The Portuguese and Spanish navigators called that great wheel of wind and current the

volta do mar. Today it is known as the North Atlantic vortex – the gyre
– famous not as a sea route but for the world of waterborne rubbish
it reels in and traps in the area the ancients called the Sargasso Sea,
because of the masses of sargassum seaweed trapped there too,
spiralled across the surface like strings of human waste, as by the
endless reel of a sewage-treatment plant, brown on blue, a striking
combination, this year's black. Year after year, winds and currents
make their unhurried round. Think of a giant tongue (not as thing
but as sensation, a teasing, graceful thrum) endlessly rimming the
asshole of the world. Turn, turn, turn, is the song, and everything
obeys. Everything returns, to precisely this spot, where New World
and Old ship their floatable disposables to meet and mingle, their
bottle tops and tampons, their Q-tips and fag butts, syringes and
lollipop sticks, in the same way and by the same routes they famously
send their eels here to spawn, and die, and hatch. *I will return* are the
first words everyone learns. The circuit that leads the eels away, north
and west, to the estuaries and inland waterways of their fathers, is
the same circuit that will one day bring them back. Everyone wants
to die in the place they were born, I've heard said. Growing up, I
often heard my mother recite the legend of a well in a distant corner
of our farm, in the townland of Carrigadrohid, in which an eel had
been living for five generations, my mother – the legend – said. That
eel could only have got there by slithering across the fields from a
lake half a mile away – a lake that had not existed when the eel or my
mother were born, either one. It was a mere stream until they built
the Inniscarra Dam. That didn't matter. There is no expiry date to
most of the orders we obey. It was written, as they say, and my mother
regularly announced the miracle to come: one day that eel would
crawl back up the walls of the well and start to trickle through the
long grass, like something washed downhill during a flood.

  Like those man-sized sturgeon in their cages, the eel too is a
dinosaur. For 70 million years, it has been living inside the same
dream, down its well. And there it waits, as far from the sea as it
ever will be. This is its lesson, which I was absorbing all through my

childhood, unawares. How to wait. How long exactly? Who knows? Who knows what makes it the right year to stir, or the right day? But one day the time for waiting is over, and the time comes to act. One day the eel stirs, as if waking from its dream, and knows it is time to go home.

All those years, biding its time, it ate everything, alive or dead, organic or synthetic, that ever bred or blew or fell or was dumped down that well. When I was a boy, I myself often threw down bottles and cans and old shoes and even once a whole tyre, just to hear the splash, and later, when my mother was sick, I threw in coins and made my wish, and after she died I threw in all the boxes of pills she left behind. But now, on the day of departure, the eel takes its very last bite, and both ends – cakehole and arsehole – shut and shrivel and seal. Which reminds me of my mother again. One day she stopped eating too.

From here on, everything goes backwards, like a film reel run in reverse. You see the eel moving – with weird, jerky motions – up out of his well, then downhill through the fields, to find the little stream by which he arrived a lifetime ago, and from there start the long journey back towards his birthplace, with a blind sense of self-importance we ourselves would do well to imitate. By day he hides. By night he threads the ditches, the phantom rivers, the misplaced lakes, in search of a seascape no less real to him than the landscape I'm now picturing for you. I repeat: in reverse. Every glimpse you catch, any time he must leave the water, the eel looks smaller than before. A little more shrivelled. A little more pale. With only one certainty: not eating, he will last longer than my mother did.

Which way to go? And how to know? By some internal compass, or by the stars? By some map tattooed in his brain, of his journey's outward leg? No. He follows gravity. Lets himself be carried downstream or downhill. Like you, he has finally learned to surrender, and once he starts he soon learns to love it, and then he cannot be stopped. No obstacle is his match. No road, no wall, no dam. He will dry-hump his way over it, shamelessly, and find the river again, every time, all the way to the estuary, to that first taste of salt. This is what he's wanted, without knowing it, all his life. With hundreds and thousands of his fellows, to be flushed like waste out into the ocean from which he came, and sucked anonymous back into the great Atlantic gyre, route of the great explorers, the slavers' silent collaborator, and final home of the North Atlantic's waterborne trash.

By now, unfed, the eels are shrunk and faded beyond recognition, almost. They look like used condoms by the time they leave the coast. As long and as milky and as flat. Already they seem too insubstantial to make their last great journey, thousands of kilometres, swimming months on end, not towards safety or sustenance but to exhaustion, to reach the place where all their kind are born, and where they spawn, and where they die. The further they go from land, the thinner and paler they get, like everything washed out to sea, so that by now, from any distance, it's hard to pick them out from the mess they're swimming in – lengths of optic cable and fishing line and floss, and orphaned iPod earphones, bud and tail, outriders for the shrivelled eels, think tadpole, think sperm, think Gathering, every wrinkled straggler the gyre pulls in, from all points of the compass, like the drawstring pucker of an old mouth. Carried on the ocean currents, they look like nothing that's ever lived. Not so long ago they were elvers, now they're glass eels again, and still the reel keeps running backwards, until they shrivel to *leptocephali*, from the Greek *leptos*, thin, delicate, slight, and *kephalē*, head. By the time they reach the Sargasso Sea, they look like nothing more than the shreds of a contact lens.

On the same current, at the same time, comes our flotilla of giant sea cages all the way from Tenerife, still full of sturgeon, each packed column still turning, turning, like something drilling down into the sea. No great leap, in my mind, to the swim tanks in which fish farmers now put wild-caught glass eels for months on end, hoping to simulate the odyssey their bodies are programmed to make, trick them into believing their life cycle is complete, they've found their way home, it's time to breed – no great leap because that's precisely the type of tank my own mother bought (the *Endless Pool,* she called it) when I was still a kid and she was still part of the eternal youth brigade. It doesn't work. They refuse to reproduce in captivity, unlike you and me. The wild eels are after something else. Even when they finally arrive (now shrivelled, remember, to little more than larvae) they refuse to stop, even to rest, they keep going, straight down, as though fleeing the light. Imagine that. Minus one mile. Minus two. Imagine that other-worldly world down there, neither Old nor New, populated by larvae, plankton, flecks of plastic, shreds of rubber, microscopic jellyfish, God knows, retch and wrack of what the brains call the Photic Zone. The French call that moult *La Neige Marine.* In English, *Marine Snow.* In the depths of the oceans, even in the height of summer, that snow falls softly on the continental shelf off Cadiz and Casablanca, and farther westwards, beneath those sea cages still moored off Tenerife, and beneath those loosed into the Canary Current and spiralling west, over the Mid-Atlantic Ridge, deep down into its valleys, and over its plains. At the ocean floor, the drifts are deep, swaddling wrecks and relics of every kind, every type of ship ever sailed or sunk, caravels and cogs, Byzantine dromon and Viking drakkar, U-boats and Greek gauloi, the silt of centuries slow-motion swallowing the hulls, the crosstrees, the mast tips. You know that joke: Bono onstage, bringing his hands together overhead, over and over, then telling the stadium, Every time I clap my hands, somewhere a child dies of hunger, and from the crowd the wit shouts, Then stop clapping your fucking hands! You know well it makes no difference, the snow keeps falling if you imagine it and keeps falling if you don't, it doesn't matter, there's nothing to see, it falls out of and into total, permanent dark, and nothing to hear, because it makes no sound. Yet how easy it is to follow. How easy – minus image, minus sound – to feel the same pull. Everything that floats or swims meets the same end, it breaks up or it breaks down, big and small, whale and plankton, and the plankton-like larvae to which our eel has now shrunk, and the plankton-like scraps of plastic and debris, down they all go, wayward and flickering, fading to grey, to black. With them dissolves and dwindles the green, solid world in which they once lived, and all hope of a future that resembles the past. On calm days, the surface is melted glass. Beneath it, the snow drifts further and further from the light, forever falling, silently, through the liquid part of the universe, and faintly falling to its final end, beyond the rival indifference of the living and the dead.

How nice that sounds. And how easy to feel you've been left behind. Which you have. You've been good. You've been listening with your eyes closed, trying to picture my every word. But now, opening your eyes, the world you saw when they were closed is gone. You are not underwater. There is no snow. You find yourself standing, instead, on the viewing platform of one of those sea cages unleashed what feels like a lifetime ago. Looking down, you can't see far, the light can't penetrate, the giant sturgeon are too tightly packed, with no obvious difference between any one specimen and the next. They're all too alike, every individual seems striking, unique and exactly the same – these magnificent man-sized fish with the pointed tail fins, the pointed head, the wicked dorsal ridge. They all look the same but they're not, the swimmers are male and female, mixed, but you'd have to be an expert – fish fanatic or marine biologist – to tell them apart, and even then the fish would have to be out of the water, and completely still, to locate all the little signs its body bears, like clues at a crime scene, to tell which is which. Imagine that scene now. Rewind the film, one last time. Rewind it all the way back to the lab. Imagine one of those prehistoric fish hoisted by pulley and cradle into the air, then laid – it takes several men to carry the thing – onto a bed of crushed ice. Watch the way the cold gets to work. Watch a lifetime's struggle flag and calm, until the creature is perfectly quiet except for the gills, flaring and pinching, like an accordion respirator by a hospital bed. An operation is about to be performed. See the stainless-steel kidney tray close by, holding various surgical tools, of the kind that terrorised your mother the night you were born. The woman leaning over the fish certainly looks a consummate professional, from the surgeon's scrubs she wears, cucumber, and the surgeon's latex gloves, and the surgeon's mask, cucumber too, gently puffing and sucking, in sync with the giant gills. She selects an instrument from the tray and, holding the thing like a pen, moves it along the underbelly of the stunned fish, as though it is indeed a pen and she's marking where best, later, to make the actual cut. But when her hand comes away you see the cut already made, and already beginning to open, like swollen lips, like a soft-centred but thick-skinned fruit – think grenadine, think passion – burst or split, and by its own ripe- or rottenness being forcibly turned inside out. But as the fish's insides seem to expand, sympathetically something swells inside you, unease growing to fear, that the internals entire are about to splurge out onto the ice, even as the gills keep up their tired gossip, like that bedside ventilator by your mother's bed at the end. The surgeon seems to feel your horror and want to calm it. At her nod, two anonymous hands close the wound the way they would a book. Then she herself takes a needle and thread from the tray. Watch her sew. She is Vermeer's lacemaker. She is Penelope. She is a fine-art restorer, and a heroic surgeon, working with the kind of care normally reserved for a gash in a famous canvas or face, doing her best to bring the severed parts together exactly as they were unpieced, with no unsightly tightness or looseness, no folds or wrinkles, no gather, no pucker, to make it an all but invisible repair.

Why cut a fish open, then just sew it up again? you might ask. What's the point of that?

It's a caesarean section, is the simple answer.

Then where are the eggs? is the question that in turn probably provokes.

The answer to that is even more simple. There are none. For the moment, everything you see is practice. It's a caesarean section performed on a male fish.

Practice for *what?* you ask.

Practice for female fish.

Female plural?

Female plural.

So male plural too?
Practice makes perfect.
Not at the start it doesn't. Isn't that the whole point?
So you lose some fish.
Male fish?
Yes.
That doesn't matter?
No.
Why not?
Because males don't lay eggs.
But you need them to fertilise the eggs, don't you?
Fertilised eggs turn into baby fish. Is babies what we really want?
How would I know what we really want? you very reasonably ask.

What we want is unfertilised fish eggs, is the answer to that. For what? To eat. Which is where these magnificent, man-sized sturgeon come in.

So why not just kill the females and take the eggs? you say, which makes me angry, which I like to be.

You've seen how big they are. Imagine how long it takes to grow to that size. Think. Every time you kill an individual, that's a whole new life cycle to start from scratch. So isn't it better to take the eggs, sew them up, put them back in the water, and harvest them year after year after year?

But what about the males? you ask. Once they're sewn up, they go back in the water too?
Yes.
Why? If we don't need them to fertilise the eggs, aren't they just taking up space and water and food?

A male presence makes the females more prone to lay eggs, and to lay more of them, and of better quality. How and why is unimportant here. The important thing is what happens when you look down into the cage again, and see everything finally coming into clear focus, indeed frighteningly so, like this year's must-have camera Christmas ad, big push, every eye, every scale, every louse, every single fish – in this and in every cage in the northern hemisphere – all wheeling clockwise, as if bound to some pitiless astronomical principle. Looking down from a great height, you see fish beyond number, or more precisely of a number the human mind can reach for but never grasp. Some are female. Some male. Of the males, some have had their bellies slit open and stitched shut again, but that is of almost no consequence, because everything you see – even here, at the eye of the vortex – is practice. The laying season is not yet quite come in, but come in it will, soon. Meanwhile the vertical columns whorl, as water whorls when being sucked down the drain. In their cages, the males have not the slightest foreboding of what comes next. Nor do you. But watch long and close enough and you will see a little red spot appear in the water. I would say, like a lone drip from an aquarelle paintbrush, but that might imply it came from above, not from within. It comes from within. It is a wound starting to tear itself apart. Keep watching and in time you see another red spot, more generous, perhaps flowering, and perhaps the first sign of protest from one of the fish. Eventually – more writhing, more red – you see that fish trailing a darker, more solid stain, and sinking, sinking, all the way down, a slow-motion explosion, even as the faithful thousands turn about it, stirring away the soil, mixing it with the falling snow. You are perhaps the least surprised of anyone at what you see, because your expectations were so few or so vague, when you started listening to me. The woman you watched perform the operation is less fortunate. Remember her – the lacemaker, in surgeon's scrubs? To her, it's more than a fish she sees come apart and disappear. She feels bad, but is not to be blamed, because the performance of such C-sections is a novelty to her and her teams. The huge quantities of equipment and fish she has charge of might seem to say otherwise, but everything – the entire industry, you might say – is still at an experimental phase. Only now that the laying period is finally coming in has she started practising the surgery she must have perfect, later, for the ladies. The surgical thread she used for the stitching is designed to hold for about seven days, then slowly dissolve. *May dissolve sooner in salt water,* the label says. That would be adequate healing for human flesh, for which such thread is intended, but is too quick for fish, whose flesh takes much longer to bind well enough to withstand the natural pressure exerted from within. The woman with the needle and thread does not know that yet. This was her first batch. One by one, then – and each time about a week after its pseudo-caesarean – the bellies of the males begin to split, tear and burst. And after a while, though still standing on the cage's walkway, the lacemaker stops looking down at them, less afraid of what she knows she will see than what she suspects she will feel. You and I can both sympathise. Nothing we ever remember or imagine feels that long ago or that far away when we close our eyes. We feel that when we open our eyes we'll be right back there in the middle of it, in its fullest confusion, like a dream where you're young again, yet feel overwhelmed with a foretaste of all the troubles to come.

The poor choice of thread came to light too late, after the operated fish were all back in their cages. Even if those cages were still anchored off the coast of Tenerife, and not adrift, it would be practically impossible to remove and redo them. The males would be too hard to identify, and catch, and extract. They are too alike. To everyone but themselves, they are not worth the trouble. In any case, there is not the time. Even in the best-case scenario, only a lucky few could be saved. In the meantime, they turn in circles – those in cages still anchored offshore, and those adrift in the open sea. That is their great duty, which they perform with such vigour, and such tenacity, and with such a remarkable absence of joy. ■

BROKEN ANIMALS

Britta Jaschinski

For the past twenty years, I have worked extensively to document the devastating lives of animals in captivity around the world, but nothing could have prepared me for what I saw in China.

In July 2010, the Chinese State Forestry Administration banned performances involving wild animals, but at many zoos and wildlife parks across the country they still go on.

Three times a day, the orangutan steps from its cage into the limelight, accompanied by a clown. Locked into obedience by their trainer's gaze, big cats go through the motions. They are drugged, and their teeth and claws are pulled out. They are controlled on stage with the help of spiked poles.

Sick and malnourished tigers pace up and down in their enclosures. Some are crippled and many lie motionless, almost too weak to lift their heads. Their deaths may be profitable – there are rumours that tiger body parts are still harvested and sold as remedies for rheumatism and impotence.

These bored, frustrated and hungry animals appear as reluctant figures in some unsolvable puzzle, or as victims of a grand experiment whose original purpose is lost in time. ■

'The Mara Elephant Project is a critical partner of the Kenya Wildlife Service in protecting elephants on the frontline and has played a key role in reducing the level of poaching and rapidly responding to human–elephant conflict in the Mara.'
— **Dickson Ritan, KWS Senior Warden, Narok County**

YOUR SUPPORT

Together we can make a difference and ensure that the elephants in Maasai Mara are here for generations to come. We need funds to expand our areas of operation to cover a wider geographical area into the remaining unprotected areas of the Mara where many elephants traditionally range.

As a non-government organisation we rely solely on the support of concerned individuals like you to help us secure a future for elephants and, as a consequence, other wildlife. **We need to act urgently.**

GET IN TOUCH

www.maraelephantproject.org

Kenya: +254 710 780215
USA: +1 317 832 8313

info@maraelephantproject.org
info@escapefoundation.org

SLAUGHTERHOUSE

Arnon Grunberg

TRANSLATED FROM THE DUTCH BY SAM GARRETT

De Rijp

In order to live, do you have to be prepared to kill? In the long run, does the will to live depend on the willingness to take the life of another in order to preserve your own?

These questions had been on my mind during my visits to war zones in Iraq and Afghanistan.

Last summer, when I made the rounds with the acute psychiatric service in Rotterdam, I asked myself how far the caregiver must go in order to keep the suicidal person from carrying out their plan.

Is living an obligation? And if so, what is killing? A necessary evil or a privilege? In order to answer those questions, or at least try to, I decided to embed myself among the butchers.

Somewhere within the quadrant 'soldier–suicide–caregiver–slaughterer', life itself must be tucked away.

As I grow older, it seems to me that the hunger for life is not so very different from the hunger for death, a hunger which apparently is in us too. The hungering itself is what it is all about; what it is precisely one hungers for is of less importance.

Cesare Pavese published diaries and letters under the title *This*

Business of Living. He wrote: 'Death will come, and she will have your eyes.'

If living is a craft, killing must be too; perhaps being dead is a craft as well.

One Monday morning at six o'clock I find myself in the canteen at North Holland Butchers, a small-scale slaughterhouse in Oost-Graftdijk, about twenty miles north of Amsterdam. The owner is Bob Bakker, a thin, sinewy man in his thirties, I would guess, with large ears and a penetrating gaze.

'Today we're going to slaughter cows, pigs, goats and sheep. No horses,' Bob says.

Sitting across from me at the table is Edwin. Edwin works for the NVWA, the Dutch Food and Consumer Product Safety Authority. He is here to inspect the animals.

'Officially, we don't talk to journalists,' Edwin says. 'We have press officers for that.'

There's no use insisting, I decide. We go downstairs, to where the abattoir and pens are located, the place where the animals wait to meet their fate. Edwin sticks a thermometer in a cow's anus. Then he shows it to Bob.

'No two ways about it,' Bob says. 'She's got a fever and is unfit for slaughter. This one's going with the cadaver disposal, to be incinerated.'

The cadaver disposal service is simply a truck that picks up the animals that have been declared unfit for slaughter.

Edwin wipes off the thermometer.

The look in Bob's eye reminds me of the look I've seen in the eyes of some soldiers. He stares off into the distance, as though he sees something behind you, and however friendly he may be, his eyes never smile.

We go out into the yard. 'There's the cadaver service,' Bob says. He points to something that looks like a truck, coming along the dyke. 'I'll give him a call.'

W e're sitting in the kitchen at North Holland Butchers. There is a can of apple and sugarbeet syrup on the table. You are allowed to smoke in here, or at least that's what Bob, the owner, is doing. Van Nelle, full-strength roll-ups.

'I've been in meat my whole life,' he says. 'I worked as a cattle dealer for a while too. Back then I sent animals out to be slaughtered. Now I do it myself. Even as a kid, I used to hang around the butcher shop.'

There are little plastic replicas on the windowsill: a sheep, a cow, a goat and a pig.

The floor shakes. 'When you hear a thud like that,' Bob says, 'it means a cow has hit the floor. Whenever I hear a sound I don't recognise, I run downstairs right away.'

I listen. It sounds as though they're operating a piledriver, but with long intervals between the blows.

Downstairs you also have the cooling cells, where the cow is transformed into steak.

'This place used to be run by an Islamic emergency butcher, let me put it that way,' Bob says. 'But I took it over about six years ago.'

'What's an emergency butcher?' I ask.

'If an animal gets hurt on the farm and can't be brought here, the emergency butcher goes there and puts the animal down and the rest of the processing happens here. That's what an emergency butcher does.'

Another roll-up.

'Listen, I respect everyone's beliefs, but the Muslims won't have their animals slaughtered here because I do pigs. So they have no respect for me. You can slaughter a sheep really well in the ritual way. You set it down on its rear end and let it lean against you, sheep like that, and then you cut it open. That's fine. But killing a cow or a bull like that, no way, not as far as I'm concerned. It's the Jewish and Muslim way, but I wouldn't start doing that, not for all the money in the world. It's inhumane.'

A cattle dealer comes in and bums a cigarette. I hear another thud from downstairs.

Bob slides his rolling tobacco over to the cattle dealer. 'I put pictures of my kids on the pack,' he says.

The cattle dealer and I stare at the picture of an almost toothless mouth that they put on cigarettes these days, to discourage smokers.

'The romance is gone,' Bob says. 'Cattle dealing and slaughtering, there's nothing romantic about it any more. *Das war einmal.*'

I realise that even for the one wielding the knife, death needs to be romantic.

Upton Sinclair's novel *The Jungle* is set in the cattle yards and slaughterhouses of Chicago in the early twentieth century. The conditions for the workers, most of them immigrants, are horrific, and so Sinclair writes: 'it was to be counted as a wonder that there were not more men slaughtered than cattle'. At the end of the novel, the hope of socialism breaks through the clouds on behalf of the lumpen proletariat.

Socialism finally won, particularly in the Netherlands. Bob's employees seem more like buddies than employees; no one mistakes a human for a cow any more.

'After World War II,' Bob says, 'we worked hard on setting up the bioindustry, because we never wanted to go hungry again. Now we're trying to tear it down. You know why some people worry themselves sick about animals? It's because people aren't starving any more. If you have to choose between a tulip bulb and a slice of bacon, you'll choose the bacon.'

I nod. After the successful spread of socialism through mankind, especially in Western Europe, it was only a matter of time before a certain kind of socialism for animals would emerge. Cruelty became less and less accepted and, even though a life without any cruelty is probably an illusion, some people feel nostalgic for the days in which cruelty and the act of killing appeared to be a necessity.

The paperwork is finished. Most of the animals waiting in the pens are declared fit for slaughter. Later on, the cadavers will be inspected as well. 'The government doesn't do anything to help me out here,' Bob says. 'They send inspectors to inspect whether the inspectors inspecting the inspectors are doing their work right.'

We go back downstairs. The cows have already been taken care of, we're now going to start on the pigs.

In a little pen, a piglet is waiting to be stunned, which means it will be rendered brain-dead.

'It's important that the heart goes on beating,' Bob says. 'Otherwise the blood can't get out.'

The sweetish odour of fresh blood is not as bad as I'd expected.

'We don't stun the pigs with the bolt gun,' says Bob. 'When you do that, they go into convulsions and haemorrhage under the skin. They get those little red dots in the meat. Consumers don't like that.'

Bob picks up the electric forceps which beep as soon as the pig is brain-dead. He places the forceps on the piglet's head skilfully, almost lovingly is what I feel like saying. If I were to be slaughtered, I would want someone like Bob to do it.

The piglet is hung on a hook, its throat is cut quickly. It spasms a few times, and that's it.

'It's no longer conscious,' Bob says. 'You can tell by waving your hand in front of its eyes. The reflexes are gone.'

I wave my hand in front of the piglet's eyes. No more reflexes.

Once a pig has been drained – that is to say, once most of the blood has run out – it's put in a machine full of hot water that reminds me of a clothes dryer.

The machine shivers. The pig's bristles are being soaked off.

A couple of minutes later the pig is removed from the machine. The smell is sickly, as though we've been making pork stock. Each animal has its own unique ID number, which means that in theory you can always trace any cut of meat. The pig's ears are cut most of the way off, leaving only its ID badge stapled to the stump that dangles to one side.

Dave, a handsome young man with impressive tattoos, starts pulling something out of the pig's feet.

'What are you doing?' I ask.

'I'm extracting the hoofs,' Dave replies. He removes the pig's hoofs the way another person might uncork a bottle of champagne.

Nothing is thrown away; I've learned that much by now. As Bob told me earlier: 'At a butcher's or in a slaughterhouse, if you ask, "Can I throw this away?" you won't be executed on the spot, but you're close.'

The pig's hoofs, however, end up on the floor. I think about taking one home as a souvenir, but decide against it.

The radio is on. A hit is blasting out above the noise of the slaughter.

The next step is to burn away the last of the bristles.

I wish that I could say: 'I love the smell of burnt pig bristles in the morning.' Unfortunately that's not true.

Then the pig is cut open and its entrails deftly removed. This morning that job goes to Hans, a man in his fifties who has been working for Bob for two years. There's another Hans too, the co-owner of the slaughterhouse. He's also helping out today.

The entrails are hung up beside the pig, because they also have to be presented for inspection. Numbers are written on the pig's legs.

The lungs, heart, liver, kidneys and spleen are beautiful, the very opposite of filthy. The way they hang there next to one another, it's like contemplating a still life. The butcher is a painter too.

After the pigs are finished, it's the lambs' turn. They are paralysed with the bolt gun, then cut open.

'If you walk around yelling, they go completely bonkers,' Bob says. 'But if you stay calm, the animals stay calm too.'

'*Fly me to the moon*,' Hans sings before applying the bolt gun and paralysing the lambs.

Wouldn't it be good for my article if I were to kill a lamb myself?

Wouldn't it be good, for me as a person, to master the craft of killing?

Today we are going to slaughter eleven sheep, two ponies, twenty-one cows and seventeen pigs.

'The ponies are obese,' Bob says. 'In France they make salami out of them, but in Holland there's no market so they're going to be pet food.'

'So why are we slaughtering ponies?' I ask.

'Their owner came down with Q fever and he can't take care of them any more.'

Today we're slaughtering Sabrina and Pebbels. Their passports are on the table – ponies are classified as horses and have equine passports. Later on, once the animals have been inspected, the passports will be invalidated with a punch, probably to prevent fraud.

It's dawn and the mist is hanging over the fields.

'Did you sleep well?' I ask Bob.

'Snuggled up nice and warm behind the mother hen,' he replies.

To him, people are animals too. What does he see me as? A fox prowling suburban rubbish bins by night?

From downstairs comes the sound of the grinder, like a heavily loaded freight elevator being pulled up slowly.

First the pigs.

'There are almost no women working in slaughterhouses,' I say to Bob.

'In the big industrial abattoirs there are,' he says. 'Polish women. Good-lookers too, often enough. What they earn in Holland is a fortune back where they come from.'

Within less than half an hour, four of the pigs are dead. I'm startled by how quickly I grow accustomed to the killing, as though I've been wading through blood, fat and entrails for years.

I know who I am now: a methodical, cultivated killer.

The only thing I can't get used to is the pop music from the radio. I would rather do my slaughtering to Tchaikovsky, the finale from *Swan Lake*.

A young man with a cognitive disability cleans the pens. Sometimes, using an electric prod, he also herds the cattle into the cage where their transformation into prime rib begins.

'It's not nice,' he says, 'but you like a nice piece of meat on your plate too, don't you?'

And there he goes, off in pursuit of another cow. She puts up a struggle.

The fragility of life is staring me in the face. It's not an easy thing to live with.

My beloved is waiting for me, back at the hotel. Standing in a pool of blood, I decide to break up with her. Then I change my mind; I want to fuck her to death. I will turn the bed into a sea of entrails, lungs, kidneys, blood and shit.

Never have I been as horny as here, in the slaughterhouse.

'I really hate the fair,' Bob says during coffee break the next morning. 'Greece is fun, I'd rather go there.'

This morning the men are talking about the annual fair that is coming to town. Around here, it is still an attraction.

A little while ago, two bulls were killed downstairs. I've been allowed to see everything so far, but not the death of the bulls. 'Those bulls were still awake,' Bob says. 'If a bull like that gets to you, he'll rip you apart. We know what we have to do, but you'd just be standing there with your little notebook. I always say: better to be a 'fraidy cat than to be roadkill.'

That's something I know about, from my days with the army. If you're not actually doing the fighting or killing, you need someone to protect you. Bob will protect me against the murderer called bull. And you identify with the person who walks beside you. Among psychiatrists I become a psychiatrist; among butchers I become a butcher. If I had been with pigs in a pen, I would have become a pig.

The dehumanisation of the other, turning the other into a thing, is a group process. Would the pigs have identified with me, too?

'A pig will eat anything,' Bob says. 'That's why you have to hang up toys in the pigpen, otherwise they'll eat each other, purely out of boredom. A farmer had a heart attack once while he was in the pen. By the time they found him, his nose, fingers and ears had been chewed off.'

'And what about sheep?' I ask.

'Rams fight to establish who's the boss. The littlest one usually wins. A smaller ram can get to the bridge of a larger ram's nose more easily, he slams it up into the skull, the bone shoots up into the brain and if the other ram dies, he's the winner.'

We go back to the abattoir.

'Some people think that slaughtering animals is cruel,' Bob says. 'But you know what's cruel? The Oostvaardersplassen nature reserve. They have cows, deer and sheep wandering around there, supposedly in the wild, where there's not even enough room for them to graze.'

After the warmth of the abattoir, the cold air of the cell where the butchering is done feels uncomfortable.

Someone once asked me: 'Travelling to war zones, Guantánamo Bay, working as a masseur in Romania, staying in a psychiatric hospital with the patients – what effect do all those projects have on you?' My brief answer was: more and more, I am prepared to do anything.

I probably won't emerge from the slaughterhouse a vegetarian, but I wonder whether there's a real moral difference between killing an animal and killing a human being.

The sociologist Johan Goudsblom wrote: 'Morality is wielding power without referring to it.' These days I would say: morality is mostly a verbal antidepressant; a story people tell each other to make themselves feel better.

My last day at North Holland Butchers. I'm going to miss Bob Bakker and his men. One can feel at home even in the slaughterhouse, on condition, perhaps, that you are not the one being slaughtered, but I'm not even sure about that. 'I'm going to Germany tomorrow to slaughter animals there,' I tell Bob. He answers: 'I have to be able to see the spire of my village church every evening.'

Hans is busy sawing the carcass of a cow in half. There's water coming out of the saw, which is there to keep the saw from burning the meat. 'You used to have cows that weighed 300 kilos,' Hans says. 'These days they weigh 700 kilos.'

Bob is working a little further along. Once again, I ask him about death's handiwork. 'You wait till they stop moving, then you grab them,' Bob says. 'Horses are sensitive.'

Is that what the predator knows by intuition? To wait until the prey stops moving, then grab them?

I recall seeing Bob pat a sheep's back before holding the bolt gun to its head. The left hand pats while the right hand kills: that must be what they mean by dying peacefully.

'Everything that comes in here has to be killed. That's the law. All kinds of animals come in here from different farms, and the inspectors are afraid of infection.'

You could also call slaughtering euthanasia.

'I prefer the meat of females,' Hans states as he goes on butchering the cow. 'Females are a bit fatter. Bull meat is coarser.'

Outside, the sunlight is dreary. In front of the slaughterhouse I say goodbye to Bob.

'I pick up the animals from the farmer myself, often enough. I used to help sometimes with catching sheep, but not any more,' he says. 'I go to the livestock markets too. I always wear a long black coat. So they know what I've come for. That used to be a tradition, you wore blue when you were buying cattle for milk production, black for slaughter.'

I feel like giving Bob a hug. The man who walks the livestock markets in a long black coat.

I keep thinking about the poem '*Die Einsamkeit der Männer*' ('The Loneliness of Men'), by Wolf Wondratschek: '*Da sitzen Männer vor einem Haus / und trinken und traümen vom Töten.*' (In front of a House the men are sitting / and drinking and dreaming of Killing.)

Neuruppin

Most of the cows here are Galloways, but they're gradually switching to Charolais. The cows are still inseminated naturally by a bull, which is uncommon and not without attendant risks. One bull, for example, recently injured its shoulder while mounting a cow and had to be put down. The butcher at Gut Hesterberg is named Detlev. The *Berliner Morgenpost* once described him as the yoga teacher among butchers. The newspaper was right about that.

With admirable calm, he leads a cow into the pen. Then he climbs a little set of steps, so the animal can't see him, and places the bolt gun against the cow's head. 'You have to see an imaginary cross between the eyes and ears. Right where the two lines intersect is where you aim.'

The cow drops to the floor.

Here I'm allowed to help out too. I removed the cow's hide. It's striking, how easily it lets go: the skin of an animal that was alive only three minutes before.

It's gentle work, in fact. It reminds me vaguely of caressing my beloved, although I usually do that without the knife.

The cow's warm paunch is taken out and remains lying on the floor. It's a wonder to see how much shit there is inside a cow.

Here at Gut Hesterberg, where only four to six cows are slaughtered each week and where they lead a natural life for as long as possible, the butchering is done in pairs. One person shovels the shit into a wheelbarrow while the other splits the cow down the middle.

Because the slaughtering at Gut Hesterberg is at such a far remove from the industrial processes now so common in slaughterhouses around the world, the killing and butchering resembles a ritual. A sacrifice is being made here, but which god has to be appeased?

In ancient Jerusalem, the priests who made the sacrifices were butchers. Indeed, Detlev reminds me more of a priest than a butcher.

The sacrificing of animals instead of humans to deities is probably a step forward, from the perspective of mankind at least, but looking at Detlev on his steps I still see a sense of guilt, at least an echo of shame. Or is Detlev just a shy person who doesn't want to be observed? I cannot help but think: God is a carnivore too.

In his book *Eating Animals*, Jonathan Safran Foer says there is no solid reason – except for sentimentality – why we should eat cows and not domestic pets. Is sentimentality a solid reason? More and more people object to the idea that killing animals is fundamentally different from killing people. Perhaps morality without the sentimentality is a kind of bookkeeping.

A cow is putting up a struggle, it doesn't want to enter the pen. When I come for a look, Detlev the butcher hisses: 'Go away.'

It takes them almost fifteen minutes to get the cow into the pen. Then it is over. 'Only a woman could be so stubborn,' Detlev says after the killing is done.

He hands me a knife and lets me cut the entrails out of the cow.

I'm not wearing gloves and the entrails feel pleasantly warm. Lukewarm.

'Do you know what that is?' Detlev asks.

'No idea,' I say.

'The spleen.'

The veterinarian arrives to inspect the carcasses. He is a hunter, too. 'The animals here are petted to death,' he says.

Later, he adds: 'The animals smell blood. They think: what's going to happen to me in there?'

In the restaurant, I eat prime rib with Karoline, whose father started Gut Hesterberg, and her husband Gerry. The first meat I've had since I started slaughtering animals. It tastes lovely.

'We actually eat meat only in a professional capacity,' Karoline says. Then she adds: 'Pork should really be banned, at least that cheap pork.'

When I leave Gerry says, 'You should come back sometime. We'll get good and drunk.'

Karoline told me that she had wanted to go and live in Berlin, but knew that leaving the cows would mean undoing everything her father had worked so hard to build. Even for these restaurateurs and butchers, cows, living or dead, and visitors are not enough. They need people like me, curious assistant-butchers.

Schijndel

'I competed in dressage and jumping, but I stopped a while back,' says Antoon Schouten, the co-owner of Schouten's Pig-breeding Farm, along with his wife, Wilma. His daughter, Yolanda, still rides.

We are sitting in the garden behind their house. It is a lovely late afternoon. There is a vague smell of pigpen in the air.

Yolanda, a biology teacher, serves us coffee. The family is receiving me as though I were a new friend.

'We put a lot of energy into producing a good cut of meat,' Antoon says. He has so much callus on his thumb that it looks like he's growing a second one.

'We have a bad reputation: we're animal abusers, polluters. These days I often don't even tell people what I do,' Wilma says. 'I don't feel like having to defend myself all the time.'

We sip our coffee.

'It's all so horribly inhumane,' she continues, 'but once they've got a pork chop on their plate, you don't hear them whining any more. Back in the old days, everyone came from a farming family. Today children barely know where milk comes from. The problem cases come to us too. The boys no one knows how to handle. They're allowed to come and work here. The farmer is the one who gets to solve everyone else's mess.'

The family owns 300 breeding sows and 2,500 pigs.

'We have a biological air cleaner,' Antoon says, which is meant to reduce ammonia emissions. 'You can go in the stalls in your Sunday best and you still won't smell of it.'

'How much does a pig cost?' I ask.

'There's a stock market price, and they pay me by the kilo,' Antoon replies. 'But for 155 euros you can take a pig home with you, except you'll have to pay the butcher another eighty euros or so.'

We walk past the pens. 'The piglets are the cutest,' Wilma says.

We stop and look at them. The sow is surrounded by metal bars, which keep her from moving freely. My attention is drawn immediately to one piglet that seems a bit crippled.

'That one's not going to make it,' Wilma says.

Maybe I can take the crippled piglet home with me and put it in the backyard at my mother's house. Does it deserve to be saved any more than its non-crippled colleagues?

'We try to keep the brothers and sisters together as much as possible,' Antoon says.

I look at the pigs. Do they know that they are brothers and sisters?

On the occasion of my visit, Antoon inseminates a sow. A nozzle is placed in the vagina. The fluid with which the sperm is mixed reminds me of dishwashing liquid.

A pair of something like large plastic clamps is placed on the sow's back, to make her think the boar's front legs are resting on her.

There is also a boar in among the sows, separated from them by a few metal bars.

'Without the smell of the boar, they won't go into heat,' Antoon explains.

Heat, a nicer word than horny.

People, too, should say: 'I'm in heat. Inseminate me now. Preferably not artificially.'

Along the walkway, I see three dead piglets in a dumpster.

IJsselstein / Schijndel

It is four in the morning when I climb into Jan van Hemert's truck. We're going to pick up pigs at Antoon Schouten's place.

'I've been doing this for thirty-five years and I started when I was eighteen,' Jan says. 'My father was in pigs too. It just comes naturally.'

We look up at the full moon.

'I've already delivered a truckload to Westfort. They start slaughtering early there, so the first pigs have to get there late in the evening.'

'Do you have a social life?' I ask.

'I always go to bed at one in the afternoon,' Jan explains. 'Then at least there's something like a daily rhythm. When I started dating I was already driving pigs, so my wife doesn't know any better. I hit the road every day, even when I'm sick. When you're in pain, it doesn't make any difference whether you stay at home or whether you're sitting in the truck. I don't go on vacation. When the kids were little we did. I've seen every Center Parcs holiday village in Holland.'

'How many pigs fit in this truck?' I ask.

'Two hundred and five. Fewer and fewer all the time, really. Animal welfare is a big deal these days.'

At around five o'clock we pull up to the pig shed.

Jan scatters sawdust on the floor of his truck. Then he picks up something that looks like a big green rattle, and hands me one too. The rattle is used to herd the pigs into the truck.

The truck has three levels, to use the space as efficiently as possible.

The open space between shed and truck is the only bit of daylight the pigs see, but it's still dark, so they don't notice that much.

'Pigs will walk towards the light,' Jan says. 'So if we turn off the lights in the shed and turn this one on, the pigs will come out by themselves.'

Before entering the truck, the pigs are given a second ear tag, in case the original gets pulled out.

I'm allowed to tag a few pigs. It's no easy task, holding onto a pig by its ear like that.

'Come on, fellows,' Antoon shouts from inside the shed.

'They're going to bump up against your knees pretty hard,' Jan says. And from the doorway Antoon says: 'Walking pork cutlets.'

That's what they are. Do the cutlets have a soul?

In among the pigs I realise that Christ did not die so much for mankind as for the pigs. The first shall be last, and in the world to come the cutlets will lead the way.

With that pious, rather Catholic thought, I feel absolved of all sins.

IJsselstein

'Look how peacefully they're sleeping,' Jan says about the pigs we unload at Westfort Meat Products.

I'm not sure that peaceful is quite the right word for it.

Using the big green rattle, the pigs were first driven into the pens, where an ingenious system of stiles then funnelled them slowly, almost automatically, towards the atmosphere-controlled elevators. In those elevators, a gas is used to render them unconscious, unlike at North Holland Butchers, where they're paralysed with an electrical current. If I were a pig I would opt for gas, but of course I've never been in one of those elevators.

Quite a few of the pigs are covered in scratches from fighting.

After Jan has disinfected his truck, I meet up with René van Rijn, a husky, helpful and competent man who will guide me around Westfort. René has tattoos that show you he works with pigs.

'What's that noise?' I ask. It reminds me of a badly tuned machine.

'Those are the pigs,' René tells me. 'We slaughter 40,000 of them a week, at two locations. A little less at the moment, because of the summer holidays. The staff here aren't allowed to wear jewellery. These days that includes wedding rings too, I think. At our competitor's, the men who couldn't worm the wedding ring off their finger were allowed to have them resized, at the boss's expense.'

The other slaughterhouse is in Gorinchem, but the plan is to close that one down once the slaughterhouse in IJsselstein has been approved by the Chinese. China is an important market for Westfort.

A veterinarian from the NVWA is keeping an eye on the pigs. He looks grumpy. Every once in a while a pig is led off to one side. Those are the ones that will be slaughtered at the end of the day, at half-speed, to see whether the animal really is healthy.

Jeroen, a young man wearing spectacles, has the job of herding the pigs to the stile and then into the elevator. The elevator goes up and down; it takes about ninety seconds. When the doors open the pigs roll out and are hung up by a back leg and then 'stuck': that is, their jugular is severed. The blood is collected. The pigs' stomachs are empty when they're slaughtered, to prevent the meat from becoming contaminated if the entrails are cut open by mistake.

Jeroen lets me take over. I drive the pigs into the stile with diligence, exactitude and even something like elation.

Half an hour later, René says: 'So now you've helped about 250 of them go west.'

I did it humanely. I didn't hit the pigs. Every once in a while, I shouted: 'Come on, guys!'

In the anime film *Spirited Away*, by Hayao Miyazaki, ten-year-old Chihiro Ogino discovers that her parents have been turned into pigs because they ate food that was intended for the gods. Walking around the new Westfort slaughterhouse, I think about that scene. There are pigs hanging everywhere – a tableau not entirely devoid of beauty – but sometimes I see people hanging there instead.

René, my guide, tells me that his hobby is dog breeding. 'Right now I'm working with an Italian breed, the *Mastino Napoletano*,' he says. 'They compete in shows.'

In one of the pens where the living animals await the rest of the process, I see a dead pig. That happens sometimes. The day before

I saw a pig come out of the truck with a broken leg. Injured pigs are stunned by hand, with the electric forceps. It squealed for a moment, then its jugular was cut. Within five minutes the blood had been mopped up.

The slaughterhouse has two sections: the machine line, where the workers wear blue overalls, and the clean line, where they are dressed in white. The machine line is where the slaughtering is done, where the carcasses are bled dry and the bristles removed. The rest of the butchering takes place on the clean line, where the animal is weighed and inspected.

The slaughterhouse is a factory: noise, conveyor belts, fairly monotonous work. There's not much automation to be seen. Many of the workers are from Poland or Cape Verde.

I watch a man as he cuts the jugulars with deep concentration. Pig after pig. Then the conveyor belt moves on. My estimate is that locating the jugular, severing it and hanging up the pig so that the blood leaves freely, with the front legs clamped between two sprockets to keep the spray of blood from dripping onto the pig, takes an average of ten to fifteen seconds per animal.

'We need to be sure that the pig is really dead before it gets to the slaughterer,' René says. 'So there's an optical sensor a little way further back, to make sure the animal has stopped moving completely.'

The only thing a robot is used for is cutting the pig in two. The robot is in a cage, for safety reasons: because the robot sees no difference between pigs and humans, it will cut in half anything that appears before its laser-controlled 'eye'. The robot's movements seem awfully human. I feel a bit sorry for the robot, having to work in a cage like that.

Today I'm allowed to hang up the pigs that roll out of the elevator by a hind leg. Strenuous work. The pigs are piled high on the conveyor and you have to be careful not to accidentally hang them up by a front leg.

'We slaughter 650 animals an hour,' René says. 'By world standards, that's more or less the maximum you can do with one slaughtering line. If you have a few lines, though, you can do more than a thousand an hour.'

Two per cent of all boars have a highly specific hormone-related smell that the consumer may find unpleasant. A Polish woman scorches a spot on the skin and another woman sniffs at it to see if the boar has the penetrating odour.

It's a wonder to see, the way she sniffs at every pig that passes. I'm reminded of Chaplin's *Modern Times*.

The department supervisor, Jan, lets me cut a pig in half with an axe and pull lard out of its carcass.

'Not easy, is it?' Jan says. 'That's what these guys do all day. And do you know how much they earn?'

'Fifteen euros an hour?' I guess.

'Closer to ten,' Jan says. 'I bet you wouldn't do it for that.'

I look around at the men. Sometimes one of them almost collides with a colleague; the conveyor belt moves faster than his hands can grab.

Oudewater

' **M** y father was good with languages,' says Rob Lunenburg. 'I thought that was so cool. I've worked in the meat industry in Italy. And in France.'

The company used to be called Lunenburg Meats, back when they still did the slaughtering in Oudewater itself. Now it's a part of Westfort, and the pigs slaughtered in Gorinchem are butchered here.

There are about 400 people working in Oudewater: Poles, Bulgarians, Czechs, Cape Verdeans and Dutch.

At four in the morning, not a minute later, the conveyors start to roll. The pigs on their hooks begin to move. The butchers in their work clothes are ready for them, the knives have been sharpened. The factory is also a theatre production.

The colours placed at strategic spots above the conveyor belt show what is being boned where. The organic pigs have already been done; there were only a few of those. The colour has been changed to yellow now, which means that the ICM (integral chain management) pigs are being boned.

During our break in the canteen, I have the impression that the Poles are sitting with the Poles, the Bulgarians with the Bulgarians.

'Later, at eight, some of them will have a hamburger,' Rob says. 'But by then they'll have a full shift behind them. And if two of them get into a fight, they both have to leave. We can't have that, not with all these knives around.'

After some elaborate hygienic measures, we go back into the plant.

An expert, in no way connected to Westfort, told me in an email: 'Robots are cleaner and easier to disinfect than people. They can also work in the dark, and in the cold.' When labour is cheap, though, robots don't pay. By email, Westfort lets me know that using robots doesn't fit in with their company strategy. 'Pork is a natural product, and a robot would have to be able to "read" a particular cut of meat. Each ham or loin, after all, is different. In this case, robotisation has not (yet) been perfected. In addition to that, many of our products are made specifically for a given customer. All customers have their own requirements. Here too, robotisation has not (yet) been perfected. In practical terms, therefore, the use of robots presents problems.' The term 'natural product' pleases me. Will there come a day when pork is no longer a natural product?

Standing next to Adri, who will be retiring soon, I get to cut away pork rind. Meat that is still warm – right after the slaughter, in other words – is easier to cut than meat that has already cooled.

'The guys who do the boning are paid by the pig,' Rob says, 'but we have a maximum limit on that, otherwise they get sloppier with boning.'

A Polish girl with bright red lipstick catches my eye. Her gaze is intense. The people here don't talk much as they work.

'Our people have to get up early,' Rob says. 'They work hard for not all that much money – we can't do anything about that. What we can do is try to keep the working environment as pleasant as possible.'

My final chore is to put pork tenderloins into boxes. This is what Libania, standing next to me, has been doing for years. She enjoys it. Her husband drives a truck for Westfort.

Sometimes I put a tenderloin in the wrong way around. 'No,' she says, 'you have to put the pretty side up.'

I am not going to leave the slaughterhouse an animal activist, nor as a vegetarian either, I'm sure of that by now. Some moralists will find that heartless of me. And perhaps it is.

No, I suspect that if I leave the slaughterhouse as anything at all, it will be as a people activist. ■

COWS | ADAM NICOLSON

I always know, when I sit down beside my small herd of cows – and also feel that they might know – that our relationship is flawed. I may be their custodian, the provider of grass in summer and hay and straw in winter, and the shelter of a barn away from the wind; but I am also their predator, the agent who removes the young bullocks at 30 months and has them killed, who has the power of life and death over all 15 of them. And so, when I am with them, that double atmosphere prevails: wary and easy, calm with a suggestion that calm might not be the whole story, all in it together but not in it together at all.

If I get up after a while, they come over to sniff where I have been, to know me by where I have sat on the grass, the young ones with their Cleopatra eyes regarding me with a mixture of what I can never quite discern: curiosity? distrust? disdain?

One of the oldest – we call her Mrs 70 because that is the number of her ear-tag – is the most trusting and comes to lick me. The cud comes up and she chews away, the pale rope-end of her tail flicking at the flies, her white tongue rasping across my clothes and hands and shoes. She looks like some kind of matriarch in a Dutch burgher household, a bony Roman nose and ridges over her eyes, but her inch-long eyelashes and the beautifully tufted tump on the crown of her head hold the memory of the more girlish years that have now long passed.

Do I love her? Not quite but I will be sad when she dies, perhaps because she seems to carry so much of the past in her. As she lies down, she settles almost camel-like, lowering her great windy bulk gently into a favourite rather muddy patch in the shade of some hazels and blackthorns, folding her front legs under her and always letting go a big sigh, more weary than contented, a great big out-blowing of the exhaustion of life. I look at her and think: never drunk, never high, never relishing the deliciousness of anything other than grass and grass and grass, maybe mixed now and then with a little sorrel or a stray orchid.

She lies there like an aubergine, one hip up, her huge swaying galleon body half floating and half sunk in the field like a fallen balloon. I look at her and remember the morning last spring when we pulled a dead calf from her womb and she licked at the body all day, wanting to summon it into life. Everything about the calf was perfect except that it was dead. I long to know what this beautiful, huge mother knew that morning. We left her with the calf and only took it away in the evening, burying it at the other end of the farm, down in the dark and the unchanging cold of the Sussex clay. ■

Emily Critchley

Home

I needed a home
so I put you in it.
I put me in it. Scientific
like an argument
about climate
change. It's the apocalypse,
dummy! Small rescue
boat: no nuclear warhead,
nothing to see here.
But no peace
at any price
      neither.

Being entwined
is such a weird animal!
Sniffing about the place, always
peeing in the same cupboard.
I've told you how many
times not to
but look you've told me
not to –
look my
pointing my gun
      again.

And now the dinner that is
burning. And the earth that is
warming. And apocalypse.
And.

Listen to the ice breaking
are you there. Listen
to the world beneath our feet
duck duck bear.
        Are you there.

Carrying around heartache
like a second baby
I will check myself
into the nearest
equanimity clinic,
sail out at the first available
promise. Need
a complete detox,
molecular fix,
to understand life
how to possibly
live in it / break it
        to my daughter.

Summer Lake, Oregon, 2014
Courtesy of the author

ON COYOTES

Diane Cook

A cross the lake in Montmorency County, Michigan, we heard the rhythmic bark of some animal. So rhythmic and so prolonged that we turned to the sound to try and make sense of it.

'Was that a dog?' my friend asked.

It was a bark to be sure. But.

'It seemed too fast to be a dog,' I said. The barks had such little space between them that I thought perhaps it could be an owl barking, thinking of the saw-whet's escalating toots and how fast they get, a bit like a bouncing ball settling down to the table.

We were just about to conjecture some more when down the shore we heard a great cacophony.

For a split second, I thought it was the loons looning out their warning call: a ghostly yodel which a few days earlier I'd almost mistaken for the bugle of an elk. We were, after all, very near the elk capital of Michigan. Just as I was about to whisper *loon*, I heard the unmistakable eerie yips of the coyotes answering back to what must have been a family member.

T here is something about the presence of coyotes that makes any place feel wilder than it is. Whenever I hear a coyote family, I get goosebumps. I instinctively look behind me, anticipating a threat. These are natural responses. I first heard coyotes answering one another when I was staying with friends in a cabin nestled on a riverbank. We thought some grisly murder was taking place. Or some witches were convening, making a potion, altering the course of history. One friend I was with (same friend as now) said, *WHAT is THAT?* We were kind of terrified and grateful for the river that stood between us and that awful, intoxicating sound.

Alternately, the ruckus of coyotes can make a wild place feel almost cozy, like home. The last time I heard them, I was at the edge of a playa at night, an empty desert basin that could house two Manhattans under its enormous star-dusted sky. When the coyotes called I felt all that expanse collapse as though we, the coyotes and I (if they'd have me), fit the space perfectly. Theirs was the only noise in the hushed night. They could have been miles into the playa but it felt as though they were whispering into my ear.

Now when I hear coyote families I feel like I'm home.

Looking across the lake, toward the sound, my friend said, 'That is so freaky.'

I said, 'I'm so glad we heard it.' I felt welcomed by the hidden coyotes even though I know they had no idea I was there, or, even if they did, they had no interest in me.

To Jack London, the call of the wolf was the call of the wild. But who among us will get the chance to hear wolves?

One summer, I lived on a small island on a Great Lake, home to two wolf packs. I regularly slept outside, in their territory, and never heard a peep, let alone that famous moan. Saw one, though. But every time I escape the city, if I'm patient, and when I least expect it, I'll hear the wild carnal frenzy of coyotes, otherworldly and disturbing, and I feel that final tether to civilization snip and fall away.

'What if I'd encountered them in the woods? I could have died,' my friend said. He'd gotten lost on the maze of snowmobile trails that carved through the woods, and had finally found some nice local women named Barb, Janet and Patti to drive him back to the lake.

I said, 'I don't think a coyote would hurt you. I think they are too small.' I hoped this didn't disappoint him.

I've lost many hours reading about mountain lions attacking people near places I love, but I'd never thought to Google how many people have been killed by coyotes.

Turns out, coyote attacks are very rare and they almost always involve children smaller than themselves. And most happen in areas where the line between wilderness and civilization blurs in increasingly complicated ways. A disproportionate number happen in California.

I remember the scene from *E.T. the Extra-Terrestrial* where the kids hear the night-hallowed sound of metal garbage cans banging together and the older brother says, 'Coyotes come back again, Mom.' And Mom immediately orders everyone inside. This became quintessential California suburban living to me – a place so newly civilized you feared the animals you'd displaced. I was just a quintessential New Jersey suburban kid (at the time). I now know that there were coyotes in the Jersey wilds, but back then I only ever encountered bats and turtles. But from that movie moment, coyotes gained their wild ominous reputation with me. Something lurking, something to be feared, even though you weren't quite sure what. It's funny how small clues in the culture can turn an unformed mind against most anything. Until you learn better. If you learn better.

The thing is that while I've heard many coyotes in my life, I can't remember ever seeing one. I know they are there. I hear them, but they never reveal themselves. And I'm the kind of person who notices animals.

I'm proud of my animal eye. I always see the fleeting dolphin fin, find the toad despite its camouflage, the hawk on the electric pole when we're speeding past. I've seen the animals of North America, the ones you would brag about having seen: bobcats in Oregon; bears in New Hampshire; condors along the Pacific Coast Highway; even a mountain lion overlooking her dominion in Point Reyes. All but the coyote. I remember their sounds, but when I try to conjure their physical form I'm left staring into the dark. Literally. I'm standing on the porch, at the edge of that lonesome playa, looking out into night so dark it feels like the Earth drops off where my porch light strains to reach.

Their calls have gotten closer. They are on the move. Toward me. Then I can hear their fur brushing the hard winter grasses. Their communal huff and whine. Their padded trot against the hard ground. I know they are standing right past the edge of where my porch light reaches, watching me from the dark side. I can hear them so close I instinctively reach for the door. But I can't see them. It's perfect. What more could you want from a wild animal? ∎

ADOPT
DOLO
THE LION

EMACIATED AND LONELY

KEPT ON A 1M CHAIN FOR 4 YEARS

DENIED HIS FREEDOM

His mane worn away by the chain

© S Taye

Now in Ethiopia at the Born Free Wildlife Rescue, Conservation and Education Centre, Dolo shares his sanctuary with rescued lioness Safia. Suffering from poor eyesight, Dolo requires expert care.

Includes Gift pack and Free Cuddly toy

Adopt Dolo for just £2.50 per month

See www.bornfree.org.uk/adopt

The mask said everything. This was a thief. A schemer and a thief. Rocky Raccoon. He arrived from Los Angeles in a small wooden box when he was three weeks old. A corner of the box was broken open and the tip of his snout stuck out, trying to get a sense of things. He looked like a drowned rat when I got him home and set him free. I felt sorry for him because everything was bewildering. He soon gave up running around the house and curled up beside me on the sofa. He deeply slept and figured things out.

Rocky grew into a fine raccoon. He was also quite decadent. He had to be woken in the mornings, he would sleep sprawled on his back like a beer drinker. His ears would literally slide down the side of his head when he slept. When you woke him and he figured out who he was, he would hurriedly arrange his ears back over his head like a lady whose wig had slipped at the vicar's. Get his eyeholes back over his eyes. Raccoons don't seem very attached to their skins. They can turn inside them like romper suits, spin round in a flash and bite. Rocky didn't bite, but he could spin in his skin.

His favourite thing was orange cake. It was also my father's favourite thing. Rocky used to mount daring and ingenious raids on the orange cake, which was subject to maximum security. I've seen Rocky clung to the back of my father's armchair, pressed flat waiting for cake to arrive in order to ambush it. He could whip away whole chunks from my father's opening mouth and run off laughing.

He also loved water. He had to thoroughly wash all his food. We sometimes got him back for his crimes by giving him sugar cubes and watching them wash away.

He got us back by discovering that toilets are waterfalls. Our house was fed by tanks on the roof. We once arrived home to find there was no water in the house. I could hear the toilet lever being pulled in the farthest bathroom down the hall. Rocky had spent the evening standing on the seat, flushing, then jumping into the bowl to cavort.

That was Rocky. An intelligent wild animal. A thief, a child, a friend. ■

Pecker was a prize from the shooting gallery at the traveling funfair, a batshit rooster that roosted in the apple tree in our yard. Pecker had the look of the just-saved, and his neck-wrung feathers, sparse, spiked, seeming wet, suited the bird's mean disposition. He was hardly a prize – more likely a giveaway at the bucket-ball stall before the carnival folk moved on. Someone must have taken the rooster for a hen and expected fresh eggs when the rooster wasn't even good at rooster things. He crowed at night and woke our mother – woke us, too. Wait for the sun, you pecker! If only he were good eating, our father said, but Pecker would have tasted foul – ha, ha. Our father, the joker, said Pecker was good for a laugh. That Pecker. His comb looked chawed and his red eyes mad. Try to cross the yard – our backyard – and he would flap down and scuttle after and peck at our legs and our feet. And it hurt – he picked our little sister's laces loose and made her cry.

Whatever happened to that Pecker?

So many figures from girlhood disappeared. All the outdoor cats that left the house and never came back, their lives cut short by – what? Dogs or cars or those mean boys on their bikes. Elmer and Homer, Sonny, Daisy, Pity, Peeps: we remembered their names. The indoor cats lived longer, but when we came home from camp, old Major was gone. All we could find was his favorite cushion, deeply indented and darkly furred. Our mother said it was past keeping, and she threw it out.

The apple-headed Siamese was so self-possessed he walked in the front door when we held it open for him, and he weaved around our legs. Sweet companion, surely someone else's pet, how was it no one ever came to claim him? We called him Charlie, but he would have come to any name. He was gregarious. He followed our father into the newly installed stairlift but was freaked by the accordion gate. At the second-floor landing, he tried to streak through it, but it sprung back fast and nearly cut him in half. Those of us home at the time watched him die.

It was that way with all the pets, and with our father, too. The Great Dane, Cavalier, belonging to our cousins, who spent a large part of one summer with us, was simply not on the lawn the next. ■

THE RAT SNIPERS

Ben Lasman

D o you and your boyfriend talk shit about me? I asked my wife over the phone. No, not really, she said. Maybe a little? I asked. A little, she said. What do you say about me? I asked. Just that you could be a lot of work sometimes, she said. It's not really about you, she added. It's more me. What I wasn't getting. My needs not being addressed. And what needs were those? I asked. I could hear the hiss in my words, like a grain of rice converting to a puff of steam. Sexual needs, said my wife.

From this line of questioning there could be no escape. I would ask awful questions until my brain uncoiled from exhaustion.

My wife was in Europe and I was in the ruins of the old apartment, surrounded by wedding presents and the clothes she hadn't taken with her. Her shoes formed a cairn by the doorway. The shower drain was still clogged with her hair. She'd been gone for two months now, but her stuff seemed to be taking up more space all the time, in a slow, moss-like creep of personal effects. Mountains of her books were toppled over in the hallway. An avalanche of unopened mail had plummeted from her desk onto the bedroom floor. Her abandoned possessions formed an ankle-high maze through which I navigated, stubbing my toes in the dark. With most of the ground covered, I had been forced to forge desire paths through the miscellanea, snaking avenues leading circuitously to the bathroom, the fridge, the sofa. My new job was sapping my energy. I couldn't motivate myself to clean up, and so the entropy of the apartment proceeded apace.

So what did you get up to today? I asked my wife. Oh, not much, she said. I went to the outdoor market and got this really delicious fish paste and some Lebanese bread and just sat outside for a few hours. I got some reading done at a little cafe. That sounds nice, I said. The question on the tip of my tongue was: How much more do you enjoy having sex with your boyfriend than you did with me? But before I went over the ledge another call came in. I've got to go, I said to my wife. Work stuff. I love you, she said. I love you too, I said, and switched to the other line.

It was Nikki Krasnik. She was waiting out front with the car. I'm here with coffee, she said. I wanted to talk longer with my wife about life with her boyfriend in Europe but I had to go shoot rats with Nikki from the roof of the Marriott downtown. I needed to make my quota for the month or I'd lose my job as a vermin sniper for the city, and I couldn't risk my life falling apart any more than it already had.

Downtown opened up like a hole in the ground as Nikki and I came over the exit ramp. Ever since the city had voted to cut off power to the street and traffic lights in the center, the only points of reference were the dull red-and-white marquee glows of the CVS, a few bodegas, check-cashing joints – the dying stars suspended in the dead center of the metro area's shrinking universe. The Marriott was the tallest building next to the towering parking garages and the empty insurance company headquarters, and even though half the hotel was closed for repairs that were never going to happen, it was still the most easily accessible roof in the area and an ideal spotters' nest, affording 360-degree views of the asphalt void around it.

Nikki was having an argument with her husband, one hand on the wheel, the other holding the phone under her chin on speaker. For $10,000 you really should have someone come and crack it open, she said. Otherwise what a fucking crazy waste of money, Bear.

Bear was Nikki's nickname for her husband, whose size, appetite and sleeping schedule were indeed bearlike, although in my experience he lacked the loping, magisterial ease and intelligence I had always associated with the genuine animal, so that at the end of the day what he most embodied was a fat, slow, mostly useless human being. He worked as a sniper too. Rules forbade relatives and romantic partners from doing fieldwork together, and sometimes it seemed like this was one of the bigger reasons Nikki had signed on. We'd been teamed up for about a month now and our kill count, while modest by the standards of the more gung-ho pros, looked positively elite next to Bear's barrel-scraping performance. The rats were big but not that big, and Bear, who was really called something like Brett or Brent, would have been challenged to hit his namesake at point-blank range with a grenade so hopeless were his aim and work ethic.

Look, Bear, I've got to hang up now, said Nikki as we turned onto the deserted main drag. We'll talk when I get home or tomorrow, but seriously don't do anything stupid before then, OK? Bear said something that sounded like potato chips being force-fed into the mouthpiece. Love you, said Nikki. Byeeee. She ended the call and dropped the phone unceremoniously into the cupholder. I cannot fucking believe this, she said. Her eyes bored through the crud on the windshield. Bear buys this ridiculous million-pound drill-resistant hard-plate safe like a year ago for fuck knows what reason, puts all our important documents in it, and today, when we need my passport for this bank thing, he has no idea what the fucking combination is, never wrote it down, and now he's talking about getting our neighbor to dynamite it down at the end of the road. I'm like really, Bear, really?

The life Nikki described with Bear often sounded so exorbitantly miserable and strange that it pushed the limits of credibility. I of course could not say for sure what did or did not go down in the Krasnik household. Nikki, at the very least, seemed to take seriously enough the unending crisis of her husband's stupidity.

OK, I was a little bit in love with her too. Meaning not *in* in love with her. Just that my wife was gone with another man and Nikki was one of the only women I knew who wasn't an old off-limits female friend, and so my mind just went there, to the gutter and the bedroom and the altar on momentary mental vacations with Nikki Krasnik. Sometimes when we were shooting from the roof, she'd pop a squat by the ledge and balance her rifle barrel on the railing to steady her aim, and I, a few feet away with my eye down the sights, would let my gaze drift over to her lower back as her jacket rode up and stare for an asphyxiating second at the lacy waistband of her underwear until I creeped myself out and had to fire a shot off just to cover up for it. Once I actually hit a rat right after, by accident. I shot into the dark and heard a startled squeak, that eggshell crack of skull and the squicky patter of rats dispersing. I must have opened up a whole nest of them.

What do you mean dynamite it? I asked. We parked in front of the Marriott, under the canopy in the bus lane. I mean Terry, this guy who lives at the end of our street, is like a demolitions expert, said Nikki. Demolitions expert, she chimed in air quotes. Will it work? I asked. She handed me a rifle and pack from the trunk. All I've got to say, she said, is if Bear paid $10,000 for that thing it better not work. Point taken, I said. I'm just going to call the safe company on Monday, she said. They can fucking deal with it.

There was no receptionist or security, so we just walked right in and took the elevator up to the roof. The crimson glow of the Marriott sign bloomed over the lip of the building. Nikki called the dispatcher to tell him we'd arrived while I unpacked our kit – three boxes of CCI Stingers, Nalgene bottles, Emergen-C and a phone charger. The shift was five hours, 10 p.m. to 3 a.m., and during it we were expected to kill at least 138 rats – or a little over twenty-seven an hour – in order to meet our quota. We all called this time slot the red-eye, not only because you always felt like you'd flown across the country the morning after, but because of the way the pulse of the Marriott letters ended up seared into your vision as the shift dragged on, tinting everything with a kind of apocalyptic rash.

You talk to Katelynn recently? asked Nikki. We lined up along the railing and began tracing the streets and jigsawed alleys below with our iron sights. A little, I said. She's out of the country for a while. Nikki knew the outline of the situation. She knew my marriage had fallen apart. She knew I was living alone. Most of the details I kept to myself since they would make my life seem more depressing than I wanted her to think. I'm doing OK with it though, I told her. Making the adjustment.

A black shape streaked across the edge of my vision. Nikki must have caught it too because we both jerked toward the movement at the same time, rifle barrels parallel. The rat was in the open now, standing on its hind legs in a leak of moonlight.

Sometimes when a rat senses you watching, it freezes, nose thrown up into the wind, raw-meat-pink paw arrested midstep. Time gagged to a halt as the animal weighed the danger of the next footfall. Ironically, it was during these contemplative pauses that the rats were easiest to kill. What are the thoughts of giant rats? I often wondered as I prepared to squeeze the trigger. I always felt a twist of guilt for taking advantage of their inability to decide, in the three-two-one countdown to the shot, whether to run or stop, race back to the shadows or bravely bolt to the nearest dumpster.

When they stand on their hind legs, arms up, wrists limp, rats can take on a beguiling sort of personhood. The bigger the rat the more real the human element. You perceive an intelligence, a sensitivity, some semblance of personality uncoiling in its twitchy rat face. You think of picture-book rats with impoverished families of hungry rat children. Rats who can cook and sail and sword-fight and work as sports reporters and teach junior high school mathematics. You press against the story of the rat you're about to kill, testing its firmness as you fight the resistance of the trigger. And then, before your partner can see you getting soft or steal your shot, you squeeze through the hesitation, absorb the baby kick and hear the achoo of the .22, and the rat, if you're lucky, snaps backward on an invisible chain, a cork of fur flying out. The body flops and checks against the curb. One, you call out, and your partner radios dispatch and updates the tally in the logbook.

Sometimes though, like that night on the Marriott roof with Nikki, you miss your opening, send the bullet wide and ricocheting. The sound sets the target off and draws out the other rats. Fuck, I said, reaching for the box of Stingers so I could reload. Rats were pouring like a thick liquid out into the street. Free-for-all, said Nikki, and we started shooting indiscriminately into the writhing viscous mass of rodents.

In cases like this the best you can hope for is a massacre. We finished the first box of fifty rounds and were about to break the seal on a second before the surge got sucked back up by the street. When there are too many rats it becomes impossible to tell if you're hitting anything. The dead fall underfoot, their bodies swallowed by the current. You have to wait for the chaos to subside before doing the count. Rats often grab some of the casualties to cannibalize later, and so I always add a couple kills to the tally in situations like this to account for the ones that get carried away and I never see. Thirty-four, I said. I've got forty-one, she said. Average it out, I said. Say thirty-nine. Thirty-nine, she mouthed as she jotted it down in the log.

Massacres are discouraged by the city because they waste resources. You use more ammunition firing on a crowd than responsibly sniping a single rat. But what happens happens, and despite the sloppy way it went down, Nikki and I were now way ahead of schedule. I took out the joint I'd stashed in the side pocket of the kit and gave her this mock-dickhead shall-we? nod. Yes we fucking shall, she said.

We propped our guns against a vent and sat with our backs pressed to the railing, passing the J back and forth. You see the way they came out back there, I said. Just whoosh, like a million of them into the street. You know what a rat king is? asked Nikki. Bunch of rats get too close and their tails get all tied up so what you end up with is like forty rats all connected and moving around like a single unit. The scariest part is that they get smarter, like proportionally to how many rats there are in the rat king. Forty rats, forty times smarter. I'd support a rat king for mayor in the next election, I said. Forty times smarter than one rat must be I'd say at least twice as smart as the average person. Ten times smarter than the guys who run this fucking city, said Nikki. Hail to the rat king, I said. Pull the lever for the rat king party. Nikki laughed, which made me smile, but also made me worried I'd have to continue to come up with new, better jokes to keep her liking me. I think this is cashed, she said, handing me the roach.

B y the end of the shift we'd come up fifteen rats short of the quota. The area must have emptied out after the surge, leaving us to take potshots at crippled and confused sleepy or drunk rats as they stumbled out to find everyone gone. It always made me feel bad, weeding out these guys. Some of the asshole snipers referred to this practice as your handicap, as in how you made up your score.

We went down to street level to tag the dead with the modified price-tag gun the city furnished for the purpose. The idea was accountability, but in reality everyone cheated. The gun stapled a red ticket with a unique number into the body that would later be compiled into a master record of rats killed. In theory this translated to one rat, one ticket, but we all knew the street cleaners that swept in after us were on a quota system too. It was their job to scan the tags, load up the dead and incinerate them. The closed nature of the system lent itself to exaggeration. It wasn't uncommon to double- or triple-tag a single rat on a bad night. The snipers and the street cleaners scratched each other's backs with this, the open secret of the rat economy.

That night we were lucky. Nikki and I found enough bodies to only have to double up a few times to reach the golden 138. We played with the idea of rounding up to 140 but then thought better of it: a clean round number always looks suspicious.

On the drive back to my house we were quiet, both because we were exhausted and because five hours spent killing animals from the top of a tall building always left you feeling a little bit like shit. The sun wouldn't start to rise for another couple of hours, and since I hadn't gotten out of bed until nearly three o'clock that day, and my schedule was already insane from trying to accommodate the six- or seven-hour time difference between my wife and me, I began to wonder if I had crossed the Rubicon into the kingdom of the nocturnal. Possums, bats and me, with my eyes screwed open from caffeine and vaguely downbeat from bad marijuana.

Nikki stopped at the end of my street. So, she said. What do you want to do? The engine of the ancient car mumbled splenetically under the hood. I mean, I don't know, I said. I wouldn't mind. As long as I'm back by like eight tomorrow, she said. Me too, I said. I mean I've got stuff to do tomorrow too. Climbing the front steps to the door, I wondered how I would play it if my wife called while Nikki was still there. It had happened before, the phone going off on the nightstand moments after Nikki had climbed on top of me. You can answer it, Nikki had said. Seriously I don't mind. But something about having a long-distance conversation with my wife about all the sex she was having with her new boyfriend while Nikki sat topless on my aching penis made me feel as if the entire world had twisted up into a crazy straw. As I let the call ring through to voicemail, I could feel sadness cloud up my insides like that blue chemical they put in pools to detect pee. One of Nikki's rules was that she never spent the night. Gotta get back to Bear, she'd say as she pulled on her jeans.

I never slept back in those days. I was miserable all the time.

I was as surprised as anyone when I heard that Bear had taken down a rat king, doing a solo sweep of the East Tower elementary school one night. My immediate reaction was that he was lying, but Nikki put that soothing thought to rest.

He was just going down the hallway with his flashlight when he heard this noise, like a hissing slithering sound, you know, like a pile of snakes, she told me three hours into a deathless shift on the Marriott roof. The only living things we'd seen in the street that evening were homeless guys pushing around rattling shopping-cart Golgothas prickling with cans and bottles, and a few stray gray wolves, which state law forbade us from killing.

It wasn't that the rats were gone. A cloud of them had chewed through the wire of my door buzzer earlier in the week, leaving just a shredded metal vein poking out of the paint by the front door. Nikki said her neighbor Terry's pit bull had been cornered in his garage by a small army of them, and had gotten pretty badly dog-eared until Terry got in there with a shopvac and sucked up the party. With downtown cleared of businesses and people, the more upwardly mobile rats, savvy to our presence on the hotel roof after the most recent mow-down, were fast relocating to less dangerous neighborhoods, in the nicer, quieter parts of town.

How'd he do it though? I asked. No offense, but I'm just kind of curious. You're fucking curious, said Nikki. What do you think I thought when he came home, middle of the night, reeking like a meat locker and like the dirtiest, literally the filthiest I've ever seen him?

That's the man I married? I asked. Something inside me flinched as I said it, a flap of skin peeling off my heart, ready for the chlorine sting of what she'd shoot back. But she just smiled. Nah, it's just Bear, she said. OMG, what the fuck? She spread her hands out in a kind of pious shrug. Here's what happened, she said.

Bear was on cleanup duty at the elementary. It's a bullshit job, by all accounts. That entire part of town had been exterminated ages ago and was actually starting to get livable again, with the new brunch place on State and transplanted baby trees going in along the side streets. What Bear did basically amounted to janitorial duty without any of the cleaning up. He roamed relatively clean institutional hallways with a flashlight and a rifle and a backpack with some basic survival supplies inside, and occasionally shot a rat or two if he was lucky.

The *Behind the Music* of how Bear killed the rat king could be summarized thus: the rat king had contracted rabies and was wandering around the hallways of the elementary school in broad daylight. It had at some point gone into a social studies classroom and gotten stuck in a closet filled with plastic bins of outdated textbooks. It was trapped for days, starved, febrile, brain-inflamed and hallucinating, and then Bear came along and killed all the rats that made it up like a daisy chain of carnival targets.

God that's terrible, I said. It's like shooting up, I don't know . . . Like shooting up a mad hallucinating hospital of rotating rats, said Nikki. Yes, I said. Exactly. I passed her the bar of expensive Bolivian chocolate I had picked up from the fresh market that had recently opened on my block. You coming to the thing tonight? she asked. I mean technically tomorrow I guess. For what? I asked. To celebrate, she said. Bear made a stupid amount of money from wasting the rat king. There's this whole payout program I never knew about. Like a bonus multiplier, you know. A bunch of people will be there. A bunch of other snipers and stuff. Fuck, this chocolate tastes like sand, she said, thrusting it back at me.

M y wife called in the middle of her night, about thirty minutes into my post-shift pass-out that afternoon. I was slowly sinking into a sweaty well of sleep with all my clothes on and my face smashed into a pile of beaded throw pillows on the sofa. The ringtone rippled like a wave of nausea through my semidream – something about my parents' house and cooking an elaborate, infinitely extending chicken recipe for Nikki – and I blindly felt in the cracks between the cushions until I made contact with the hard plastic vibrating noise-making box. Hey love, I said. How are you doing? Oh my God, she said. I think I'm pregnant. It sounded as if a helicopter was landing behind her. Where are you? I asked. Bathroom, she said. What's that noise? I asked. The light bulb, she said. Isn't it loud? Yes, I said. Very.

Before we had ever had sex, back in college when we had first started spending time together, my wife had told me she was extremely, almost excessively fertile. The Russian in me, she said. Me and my mom and grandmother are all baby factories. I asked her how many children she had had. Zero, she said. But I did have to take the morning-after pill a few times. And how many siblings do you have? I asked. Just me and my brother, said my future wife. So far her familial claim to supernatural fecundity seemed pretty shaky. Sensing my skepticism, she promptly swerved in front of it and elaborated. My mom had eight brothers and sisters though, she said. Plus another two who died. That's a lot, I said. And my mom got three abortions, she went on. One right before my brother, another like three months after my brother was born and then again like immediately after me. Wow, I said, totally unsure, as a twenty-one-year-old man, what to say or how to respond to this information. How do you feel about that? I asked. I feel like if we're going to see how this goes going forward, she said, then I'm going to need some serious birth control. She rolled over in the tiny dorm-room bed we were cuddling on, propped her elbows on my chest, balanced her head on top of her hands and looked down at me with a sage and pitying expression. Honestly I don't think we should do anything until I've got my uterus locked down, she said. Too risky, right? College couple baby mama drama? No thanks.

Why do you think you're pregnant? I asked her, wresting myself from the sofa and its promise of oblivion. Well because I haven't gotten my period in thirty-five days, she said. Who's the . . . I hit a wall, but she helped me over. I know who the father is, she said. We listened to the background hum on the call for a while, this thin loop of drone unpeeling over and over. It's not you, she said. Don't worry.

I had the computer open, so I scrolled through some things without understanding any of them because my brain was on fire, trying to climb out of my eye sockets and escape to the bathtub to drown itself. The point isn't whether I worry or not, I said. I wasn't even talking at that point, just fogging bullshit out my mouth. Forget insincerity – what I was saying was immaterial, substanceless, a mist to fill that Plutonian telecom space between our earpieces, which were 3,000 physical miles apart. With each scratchy repetition, the texture of the long-distance background hum deepened and fractalized, drawing me down into its branching, caverning passageways.

I don't know what I'm going to do, she said. What do you mean? I asked. Look, this is not a straightforward issue for me, she said. As a woman and a feminist, part of me says this is a terrible time for this to happen and it's just adding complication to an already complicated situation. She laughed. And then part of me, a very real part of me, says I do want it. In the silence that followed, I pictured my wife as the new mom holding a baby in a watermarked stock photo, the room a hyperbaric white, the child smiling and reaching up for its mother with Michelin-man tire arms. So what's going to happen? I asked. What are you going to do? I don't know, she said. I seriously do not know. Did you talk about it yet? I asked. You and your boyfriend. No, not yet, she said. You're the first.

I felt I understood. Not the real reason, not the motivation untwisting in her head. That I couldn't know. But there was strange comfort in finding myself atop the hierarchy of the need-to-know in that moment, like the subtle pressure of a finger tracing down the pegs of your spine. I understood then that if I were the pregnant one, abroad with my new boyfriend, and she were me, living alone in our old home in this derelict and forgotten corner of the American Northeast, she would also be the first one I would call.

Can we talk later? she asked. Will you be around? I'll be out, I said. But I'll pick up. The hum on the line cut out abruptly, leaving us alone together at last. Our staticky breaths flared in the earpiece like the mouths of sea anemones. I love you, I said. I love you too, she said. Then the hum came back, whinier and more insistent, with an electroshock gargle running underneath it this time. It was the signal to go. The talk was over.

After charging my phone up to 50 per cent, I put on my coat and boots and headed over to the Killcreek, where Nikki and Bear and everyone else were meeting up, and I could drink on the rat king tab until my mind collapsed in on itself like a forgotten kids' clubhouse hidden deep in the woods.

I accidentally overdid it almost immediately on boilermakers and bad conversation at the Killcreek, enough so that after one hour I wanted to leave – preferably with Nikki, who, I had to keep reminding myself, was the wife of the guy the party was for. She was playing nice for all of Bear's awful friends by ignoring me at the other end of the bar.

The big man himself was having the time of his life. Whenever I looked over I'd see him taking group selfies with a rotating gaggle of snipers and girls and bar employees. He was flagrantly underdressed, in sky-blue gym shorts and a T-shirt from one of those online T-shirt stores, showing silhouette dinosaurs walking around with ghetto blasters, passing prehistoric blunts. THE STONED AGE, read the text on the shirt. There were so many things wrong with the picture I didn't even know where to begin. On top of this he wore a gray linoleum-colored blazer with pasty white-guy flesh-tone elbow pads. While I was processing this calamity of an outfit, some girls came over and gave him a headband with plush bear ears on it. He gave them all squirming bear hugs and put on the gift, crowning himself. The Bear King. All I wanted to do was talk shit with my wife about it, text her you would not believe this. How late was it where she was? I tried to do the math but my brain locked up and so I figured fuck it, the need to do this almost certainly unnecessary thing would pass.

Francis to my left was showing some of the other snipers pictures of the dead rat king. I got into the huddle around the phone. It's insane the number of rats, Francis said. All different sizes. The images hit my eyes like high beams as he thumbed through them. Look, this guy was eating the dude next to him when it got killed, said one of the snipers. Francis pinched in on the photo and we saw that it was true – the rats had been cannibalizing one another, neighbor gnawing neighbor in an oily whirlpool on the floor of the textbook closet. I thought of Charybdis, snacking on itself. The rat tails were knotted and kinked together in the center of the circle like eggy bucatini. Thing looks like the alien from *Aliens*, said another sniper. The face-hugger alien, you know? The circle hummed in agreement.

After another few drinks I couldn't be social anymore, so I went to the back of the bar and put a few quarters into the Buck Hunter machine. I was partial to the exotic options, and went with wildebeest for game. Back when the rat sniper jobs first opened up, me and my wife would joke about how all the time we put into playing Buck Hunter at bars meant we'd make excellent shooters. We had extensive training on the simulator. If worse comes to worst, she said.

She'd left me, I'd become a sniper – not the best one and not the worst one, and the worst one had just nabbed the grand prize of all the snipers. I could not tell, standing under the red lights of the Killcreek, aiming a lime-green plastic gun at a pack of video wildebeest, with Nikki and Bear putting on the married pageant in the main room, if this, this right now, was the worst it could get. You never can is the thing. Don't get too optimistic, I told myself.

Shoot the birds, said Nikki. She'd snuck up behind me with two beers. Maybe the world wasn't so bad after all. You missed them, she said, setting the drinks down on the table by the arcade cabinet. They're gone now. How's your night been? I asked. She fed some coins to the machine and pulled the second-player gun, traffic-cone orange, from its holster. Oh, it's all right, she said. Bear seems happy. He does, I agreed.

We silently wasted computer models of endangered species for a few rounds. The screen flashed with shots and the fake animals blew backward, blinked a few times on the ground and disappeared. Nikki was outscoring me by a few wildebeest, plus a couple of bonus cheetahs and birds. But I was barely trying, and performance seemed beside the point. I was grateful for the company, the shoulder-to-shoulder proximity, the fact that if I wobbled a little to my right my arm would make contact with another arm, both crooked to cradle the butt of a plastic rifle, barrels in parallel aiming at animated shapes on the arcade screen.

Katelynn thinks she might be pregnant, I said. Thinks? asked Nikki. I could hear her eyebrow raising. She really was such a good friend. She doesn't know for sure, I said. She told me she hasn't gotten her period in more than a month. Do you think she's fucking with you? asked Nikki. I just don't understand why she feels she has to tell you that. I understand, I said. Or I feel I understand even if I can't say what exactly I'm understanding. I just understand it the way you understand if you've got a cold or you feel depressed but don't know why. It's a sense kind of thing more than anything else. So you have a sense that you feel you can understand why she might be sharing this piece of information with you, said Nikki. Exactly, I said.

A herd of wildebeest was stampeding across the screen, galloping in algorithmic eddies as they wound out of the frame to safety. I didn't know enough about computers to say whether the wildebeest who escaped did so for good, or if the code that made them up was simply recycled for the next session. It probably was, I figured. Digital wildebeest reincarnated as digital wildebeest, running and getting shot on the same fake Serengeti forever. Buck Hunter can feel like proof we are all living in hell.

As the round ended, Nikki put a bullet through the kneecap of a large female wildebeest charging for the perimeter. The heifer spun, clipped into a baobab tree and got stuck there, flickering. The texture of its hide and the texture of the bark scissored into each other, juddering as the math under the hood of the arcade machine spun in circles. The timer at the top of the screen climbed toward 99, hit it, and then the game froze except for the wildebeest, which stuttered and struggled against the surface of the tree. Nikki and I fired our guns at the screen for a while, trying to put the pinioned animal down. We pressed the coin-return button and pounded on the walls of the cabinet. Nothing worked. The only option left was to pull the plug and reboot the Buck Hunter universe from scratch. But we decided not to do that. Should we just do what we're going to do anyway and use this as an excuse to get out of here and leave it like this? Nikki asked. I nodded. We drained our beers, put our guns back and snuck out the fire exit.

I had one hand up Nikki's shirt and the other down the back of her pants when I felt her phone vibrate in her pocket. She pushed off me and scooted to the other side of her car's back seat. It's Bear, she said. You mind? No, no, take it, I said. It's totally fine. We were parked in a dirt turnoff about a mile up the road from Nikki's house. Sometimes you'd get a rotating cast of teenagers' cars staking out the spot, daddy's BMW with the windows fogged, the antediluvian Saab belching dub music and synthetic pot smoke from the open sunroof. But tonight was a school night, and Nikki and I had the place to ourselves.

You're where? Nikki said into the phone. Doing what? She cupped the mouthpiece and dropped her eyes at me. They're going to blow up the safe, she shout-whispered. They're all coming over from the Killcreek. Yes I'm here, Bear, she said. Yes, I'll meet you down there. Bye. Yes. Bye. Jesus Christ, she said as she clambered up into the driver's seat. You want to go see some losers fail spectacularly at something that was already a terrible idea to begin with?

Nikki's road ended in the salt marsh. The pavement didn't even stop, it just ran into the turbid water. By the time we got there, a half-dozen cars were already circled up at the landing, the silhouette of the tailgates set against the bonfire. Nikki parked a few meters away. Go out the trunk, she instructed. Just because, you know. She got out and walked toward the flames and the people, and after I felt she had put enough distance between us to deflect suspicion, I let myself out of the back and headed down to the water as well.

The night was calm and chilly, the marsh rippling with bands of moonlight that stretched and shrunk with the motion of the waves. The chatter of the crowd matched the volume of the incoming tide, the rustle of voices and raking sand and stones blended into a wash.

Bear, still in bear ears and lino jacket, was standing in the center of the snipers, hammy fists on meaty hips, watching the blaze. Nikki came up beside him, kissed him on the cheek, and he put out his arm and tucked her into him, so that against the blur of heat and smoke and dark they looked like a single two-headed person. In the firelight, I could see a man kneeling by a big black box. That must have been the safe. If Bear had died and been reincarnated as a safe it would likely have looked like this one: squat, thick, confoundingly secure. The man who must have been the neighbor, Terry, was attaching gray globs of putty to the outside of the safe and running wires inserted into them out to an open suitcase filled with buttons a little ways away, behind some rocks.

I entered the crowd, caught a few heys and wassups, and positioned myself beside Bear and Nikki, because it was directly downwind from the smoke and nobody else would stand there. Hey buddy, said Bear, recognizing me. Don't your eyes sting? No, it's OK, I said. The wind will move eventually.

I felt my phone go off in my jacket. One sec, I said to Bear and Nikki. Gotta take this. I retreated to the perimeter of the crowd, moving toward the edge of the forest. Wobbly light from the bonfire danced against trees, my shadow widening as I drew closer. I put a finger in one ear to mute the background noise and crouched in the gravel. You there? I asked. I got it, said my wife. We're clear. All clear? I asked. All clear, she said.

Feet started scurrying behind me. Everyone was heading behind the rocks. Look, I love you, I said to my wife. How are you doing with all this? We can talk about it later, she said. It's the morning here and I overslept and now I've got fifteen minutes to get to this thing. Totally, I said. Of course. The detonator squish-hissed behind me. The voices cut out. I turned around.

In the end the explosion was disappointing, more smoke than fire and flaming bits going all over the place. The safe just wobbled a little and didn't open, heated up to the point where you couldn't touch it. We stuck around until the tide came in and hit it and steam shot up in this beautiful fountain all around it. It really was something to see, with the steely water and the cotton-candy shreds of dawn coming through the gaps in the clouds. They wound up just leaving the safe out there by the end of the road after that. No one ever went to get it.

In time the ocean claimed the safe and the personal documents of Nikki and Bear, and my wife broke up with her boyfriend and moved back to the city to open up a small shop in a nice part of town recently freed of rats, selling expensive spreads and cookware sourced from contacts she'd made in Europe. After a trial reconciliation she and I made our peace and divorced, and I moved out to Los Angeles and pretty much lost touch with all those people. ∎

© ALAN BAKER

THE KABUL MARKHOR

Nell Zink

The Kabul markhor looked out of his window and saw that it
was snowing. It was a windy spring day. The wet flakes swirled
and clung to the tree branches. He felt very lonely after spending
the winter holed up in his cabin eating Doritos. He decided it was
time to go to the store for some salsa and maybe go visit Bob. Three
beers aren't too many to drive on when you weigh three hundred
pounds. It took him a while to get the jeep started, but just when he
thought he'd flooded it for sure, it lurched into gear. There was almost
a mile of steep, sandy ruts before the main road. It seemed like there'd
been a lot of erosion over the winter. His horns clattered against the
roof as he bounced down the driveway. That was the last thing he
remembered.

He woke up in a bright hospital ward. There were blinding lights
everywhere and green curtains around him. Nothing hurt. He wasn't
bandaged, and he could move his legs just fine. His head felt heavy,
though, and everything seemed distant, as if it didn't really concern
him. He wondered if he'd been drugged. He thought absently about
the car. He heard footsteps and called out.

A nurse came through the curtain. She asked what he wanted. He
asked where he was. She said, 'Washington.'

'And what hospital is this?'

She looked surprised and said she'd get the doctor.

The doctor came in. He had a double-breasted suit with pinstripes, and a tie tack with a panda on it. The Kabul markhor felt a sudden tightness in his throat at the sight of the pin, and realized with a horrible shock where he was. He sat upright. The doctor extended his hand to pat his nose.

'Don't pat me,' said the Kabul markhor.

'Excuse me?' the doctor said, offended.

The Kabul markhor, whom we'll call Fritz because his actual name is kind of a snorting sound, jumped to his feet right on the bed. He swung his head around, enjoying the way his heavy spiraling horns cut the air. The doctor jumped back and jabbed at a little buzzer by the bed. Fritz bounded from the bed right over a curtain rod and started for the door. It said EXIT in big red letters, but it was locked. He turned to face the doctor, who was walking toward him and rubbing his hands together greedily.

'It's okay, it's okay,' the doctor said, 'you're in good physical health, and that's what matters.'

'Where's my car?' Fritz asked. As his head cleared he was realizing that there were lots more questions he needed answered, and added, 'What am I doing here? What's going on?'

The doctor suggested that he get back in bed.

Fritz said, 'I'm not tired.'

'But there are other guests here who need their rest,' the doctor said. 'Perhaps we can go to my office.'

He opened a side door and led Fritz down a long, quiet hallway. It was lined with dozens of tiny doors through which Fritz could make out the agonized moans of weasels, skunks and badgers trapped forever in the last stages of depression. He felt nervous. By the door was a little manger stuffed with hay. Fritz paused for a nibble but the doctor motioned for him to take a seat.

'I know you must have a lot of questions,' the doctor began.

Fritz nodded.

The doctor munched from a bag of chips on his desk. He explained that the jeep had turned over and been totaled, and Fritz had been taken by helicopter in a sling to the zoo. They'd spent $45,000 nursing him through a two-month coma, and as they knew he didn't have much money, they proposed to employ him in the exhibition area for four and a half years. Furthermore, $10,000 a year was a good salary for a Kabul markhor.

Fritz was calm at first. 'You know, I doubt I was at fault – I mean, I'm a good driver. Was there an investigation?'

The doctor took another handful of chips and said nothing.

'You can't just keep me here.'

'Sure,' the doctor said. 'Try to leave. You owe us $45,000 and you're broke. I'm not writing off $45,000. I have a zoo to run here. In addition, I hear there was an open bottle of Metaxa in the car.'

Fritz started, vaguely remembering a drive-in movie with a certain Persian lamb. He was sure they'd finished the Metaxa. 'I want a lawyer, right now,' he said, lowering his head.

The doctor pulled a cattle prod from his desk drawer. 'My friend,' he said, 'I assume you know your rights.'

This was a standard phrase people used before giving animals the shaft. Fritz had heard it from loan officers when he bought the cabin and from that hotel clerk in Aspen before he spent the night on the roof. He looked gloomily up at the cattle prod, thinking it would be good to know if there were batteries in it before he came any closer. The doctor's look darkened and he pulled an old revolver out of his coat and aimed it at Fritz's forehead.

'Kneel down,' the doctor said.

Shit, Fritz thought.

The doctor rang a bell and two flunkeys came to put a halter on him, struggling to fit it over his tremendous horns. They led him through back alleys to the exhibition area and put him in with two gerenuks. He tried to protest but the flunkeys just kept saying, 'Shhh.' Then they slammed the iron door in his face.

He started to address the gerenuks, but they seemed retarded or something. They just kept running over and over back and forth in the pen. He heard the low, familiar bellowing of Ankole cattle, but they were speaking Kinyarwanda. 'Anybody?' he called out, but as far as he could tell there was no one within hearing who could talk to him. He lay down on a pile of straw and watched the cretinous gerenuks scamper in endless circles.

The next morning the zoo opened for business. He wandered out to the railing and scanned the crowd. His sole hope was to see someone he knew. Every day was the same. He kept watching the crowd. He was afraid to leave the area near the fence in case one of his friends happened by. He must have asked 10,000 people, 'Please, for the love of God, just call Bob for me –' but they all ignored him. He began to think he was losing his mind. 'Why don't they pay attention to me?' he thought. He didn't know there was a sign on the railing that said, PLEASE DO NOT FEED OR LISTEN TO THE ANIMALS. COINS AND OTHER REFUSE CAN KILL THEM, AND THEIR REQUESTS ARE SELFISH AND ILL-ADVISED. Once someone threw him a Cheeto. He yelled back, 'Hey! Call Bob for me! Write down this number –' but the person looked guilty and ran away hurriedly.

A year went by and his bitter scowl became permanent. He habitually butted the side of the shed until his horns had latex paint chips stuck in them all down their fronts.

In the spring of the second year, a young woman came to the zoo. She stood at the railing, looking furtively from left to right, and Fritz watched her absent-mindedly, grinding his teeth. When everyone else had moved on, she suddenly leaned over the railing and said, 'Hey.' Fritz snorted. 'Talk to me,' she said. 'Do you know English?' Fritz snorted again. He'd long since made up his mind that humans were a waste of time. She said, 'I believe in your civil rights. Just let me know if you can understand what I'm saying.'

He said, 'Just please call my friend Bob for me.'

She smiled and began hurriedly. 'Have you thought of civil disobedience? Break out. They can't keep you a prisoner here – what are they gonna do? Shoot you in front of hundreds of people? The ACLU takes cases like yours. There are things you can do.'

'Listen, sweetheart, these people can buy and sell me –' he cut himself off mid-sentence as a couple with a baby in a stroller wandered up.

He snorted loudly and coughed a few times. The family laughed. When they wandered on, he continued, 'I'm out of here in three years. I don't want to die here. I'm into them for $45,000. I'd get about two blocks. What you can do for me is call my friend Bob in West Virginia. Do you have something to write with?'

'I'll be right back,' she said, and walked away.

He heard a little popping noise and saw her fall to the pavement. The doctor's flunkeys ran up, dressed as medics, and put her on a stretcher. Then they started off toward the Great Cat house, but not without first giving Fritz some very meaningful looks.

Just then his friend Bob strolled up. He couldn't believe his good fortune. 'Bob, man, what the hell took you so long!'

Bob rolled his eyes. 'They've got you down as a mouflon, man, what was I supposed to do? They got your name wrong, they had you in with gerenuks. I've been to zoos in fucking Taiwan looking for you, so don't tell me –'

The doctor's flunkeys were coming back with the dart gun.

'What the fuck?' A dart hit Bob in the neck and dangled there.

Bob was an African elephant. He socked them in the head with his trunk and then knocked down the wall of Fritz's enclosure. They ran to the parking lot, jumped in Bob's Land Rover and drove away. They stopped at the first 7-Eleven they saw and got Big Gulps and Doritos and took off for Bob's huge underground complex from which he controlled the Federal Reserve.

Fritz discovered he'd lost weight in the zoo and no longer suffered from hypertension. His fleece was much thicker from all the time outdoors, and really he'd never looked better in his life. Bob lent him his VW Thing, which he never drove anymore because he thought convertibles were too dangerous, and at the next 7-Eleven Fritz exchanged phone numbers with a cute chamois in a VW Beetle, who obviously thought they had a lot in common. He was on cloud nine.

The authorities, of course, were looking for a mouflon. He got right past the roadblock on the way to his house. When he arrived, he found that a group of owls had moved in and made a lot of improvements, including grading the driveway. They left in such a hurry they didn't even take their cases of beer, which filled the basement. 'You know,' he said to Bob one day about two weeks later as they lay in hammocks on the porch drinking Pabst, 'I really thought my life was ruined. I thought I'd never get over that zoo thing.'

'Yeah, it's funny,' Bob replied. 'I thought the same thing when I lost the Soviet Union.'

Fritz sighed and drifted off into a peaceful, drunken sleep. ∎

A MOVEABLE BEAST

Helge Skodvin

Introduction by Ned Beauman

Even long after death, animals can still be displaced by habitat loss. In 2013, the University Museum in Bergen, Norway, was closed for renovations and its collections were moved into temporary storage. Photographer Helge Skodvin, who visited the museum regularly as a boy, was given permission to document the migration of the natural history department. The curators had to take great care with their charges, some of which are over 150 years old and as unwieldy as they are fragile. It took seven burly men to lift the stuffed African elephant onto a pallet, although in these photos no humans are seen, only taxidermy idling in transit.

It is alarming to think that some of these stuffed animals may one day be valuable as more than just visitor attractions or artefacts in the history of Norwegian science. After all, in the same way that the death of an artist will boost the prices of his or her work, the extinction of a species will elevate, and sanctify, any preserved specimens. In this sense, taxidermy offers animals both a second life and a second harassment by the Anthropocene. Their rest can be disturbed not only by the movers but also by having new significance suddenly thrust upon them when a forest is razed thousands of miles away.

At present, human activity is obliterating dozens of species every day. The Bornean orangutan, for instance, seen here gazing at real trees from its perch on a merely illustrative one, may be extinct in the wild within the next ten or twenty years; after that, it will live only in the twilight of captivity, and in the long run, who knows? The last sighting of a live dodo was in 1666, but the last demise of the taxidermied dodo was in 1755: that century-old stiff, known as the Oxford Dodo, was so rotted that it had to be burned by the curators at the Ashmolean Museum. Those curators had no inkling that they were cremating the last of its kind, because it wasn't until the end of the eighteenth century that naturalists even began to conceive that it might be possible for a species to go extinct.

Just imagine that state of innocence! When you could wake up in the morning without the awareness that your every action, indeed your very existence, is an act of violence, a tiny and indirect act of violence but nevertheless a constituent part of a communal, relentless, irreparable rampage against the best, most beautiful, most interesting collection of things in the galaxy, conducted by a mob whose only real justification for existence in the first place is their unique ability to appreciate those things. Today we are painfully conscious that any of these exhibits may one day be precious, just like the Oxford Dodo. The famous Room of Endangered and Extinct Species at the Grande Galerie de l'Évolution in Paris may one day become the paradigm of all the natural history museums in the world.

People who devote their lives to animals – even to dead ones, as the curators of the University Museum of Bergen do – are more or less exempt from shame. Nevertheless, when we observe the care with which a shark is swaddled in bubble wrap or a moose is craned over the street, these expressions of reverence and consideration towards the animal kingdom seem poignant because they are so insufficient, so belated, so haunted with guilt. When we treat our specimens like this, it is as if we are giving a gentle sponge bath to the somnolent body of a child we ourselves have beaten half to death. ∎

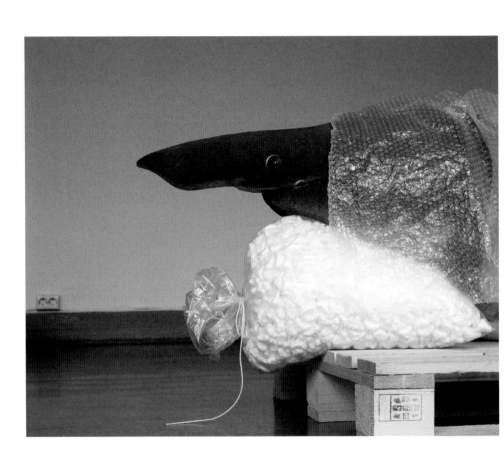

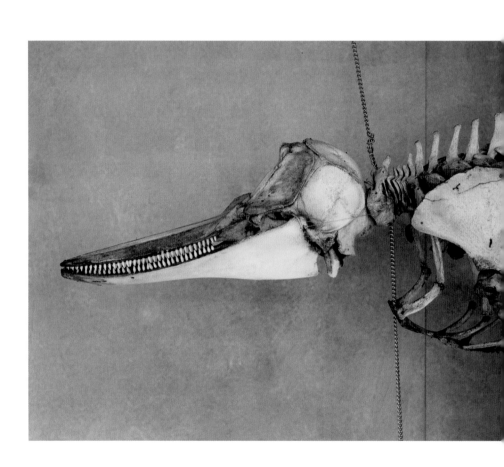

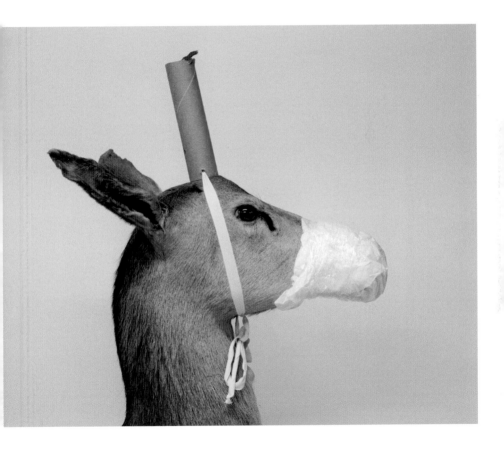

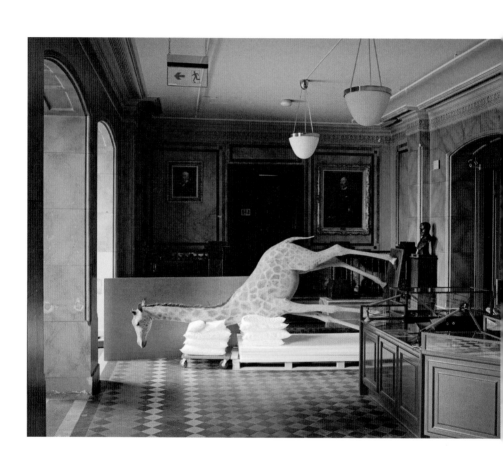

G

SWIMMING COACH

Anosh Irani

When his brother told him that he should read a short story by an American named John Cheever, Ulrich immediately thought of at least ten better ways to spend the evening. He could gather all the two- and five-rupee coins scattered in different corners of his room and go downstairs to the Irani restaurant and exchange them for paper currency. He could go to the laundromat across the street and finally collect his socks and underwear.

Or maybe he could just stay put. Why do anything? The smallest of his movements would add to the mayhem. Clare Road was a gaudy mix of hair salons, coffin makers, churches, cheap boutiques, and – worst of all – schools. Those screaming brats had managed to hijack Clare Road. Now everyone and everything had that unbearable quality that most children have.

'Just read the Cheever,' said Moses. His brother was still looking for the key to his motorcycle, which Ulrich knew was lying on the floor, at the foot of the table. 'This guy, this loser American rich type, he's at a pool party, and he suddenly decides to swim all the way home through people's backyards.'

'How the hell do you swim through a backyard?'

'Through their pools, yaar. He's tipsy and decides to go pool-hopping. But that's not what the story's *about* . . .'

153

GRANTA

THE MAGAZINE OF NEW WRITING

PRINT SUBSCRIPTION REPLY FORM FOR UK, EUROPE
AND REST OF THE WORLD (includes digital and app access).
For digital-only subscriptions, please visit granta.com/subscriptions.

GUARANTEE: If I am ever dissatisfied with my *Granta* subscription, I will simply notify you, and you will send me a complete refund or credit my credit card, as applicable, for all unmailed issues.

YOUR DETAILS

TITLE ....
NAME ....
ADDRESS ....
POSTCODE ....
EMAIL ....

☐ Please tick this box if you wish to receive special offers from *Granta*
☐ Please tick this box if you wish to receive offers from organisations selected by *Granta*

YOUR PAYMENT DETAILS

1) ☐ Pay £32 (saving £20) by direct debit.

To pay by direct debit please complete the mandate and return to the address shown below.

2) Pay by cheque or credit/debit card. Please complete below:

1 year subscription: ☐ UK: £36   ☐ Europe: £42   ☐ Rest of World: £46

3 year subscription: ☐ UK: £99   ☐ Europe: £108   ☐ Rest of World: £126

I wish to pay by ☐ CHEQUE   ☐ CREDIT / DEBIT CARD

Cheque enclosed for £_____ made payable to *Granta*.

Please charge £ _____ to my: ☐ Visa ☐ MasterCard ☐ Amex ☐ Switch/Maestro

Card No. ☐☐☐☐☐☐☐☐☐☐☐☐☐☐☐☐

Valid from (*if applicable*) ☐☐ / ☐☐   Expiry Date ☐☐ / ☐☐   Issue No. ☐☐

Security No. ☐☐☐

SIGNATURE .... DATE ....

Instructions to your Bank or Building Society to pay by direct debit

BANK NAME ....
BANK ADDRESS ....
POSTCODE ....
ACCOUNT IN THE NAMES(S) OF: ....
SIGNED .... DATE ....

DIRECT Debit

Instructions to your Bank or Building Society: Please pay Granta Publications direct debits from the account detailed on this instruction subject to the safeguards assured by the direct debit guarantee. I understand that this instruction may remain with Granta and, if so, details will be passed electronically to my bank/building society. Banks and building societies may not accept direct debit instructions from some types of account.

Bank/building society account number

☐☐☐☐☐☐☐☐

Sort Code

☐☐☐☐☐☐

Originator's Identification

9 1 3 1 3 3

Please mail this order form to:

Granta Publications
12 Addison Avenue
London, W11 4QR

Call +44(0)208 955 7011
Visit GRANTA.COM/SUBSCRIPTIONS

Tiger Mask, 1972
Courtesy of the Victoria & Albert Museum

TYGER, TYGER

Aman Sethi

A man-eating tiger was on the prowl when I arrived in Pilibhit one rainy evening in September. It had killed three people in four days in August, then escaped into a sugar-cane field in nearby Himkarpur where – a month later – it was presumably still holed up. A forest department team armed with tranquilliser guns was camped out on the fringes of the field, but the rumour was the big cat had given them the slip.

Tigers had killed nineteen people in ten months in Pilibhit, a largely rural district in the northern Indian state of Uttar Pradesh. Each passing death had led to increasingly violent confrontations between the grieving villagers and the hapless district administration.

The forest department was inundated with so many phone calls reporting tiger sightings that they had taken to maintaining an *afwah* – Urdu for 'rumour' – register. In one instance, a ranger told me, a senior administration official reported tiger pugmarks outside his residence: on closer examination, these turned out to be the paw prints of a pet dog. Everyone was afraid.

Uttar Pradesh's chief minister, an inept saffron-swaddled priest named Yogi Adityanath, had flown down to Pilibhit for a day to hand out cheques for 500,000 rupees to the families of the most recent victims and to assuage fears that the district was overrun by rampaging maneaters. In a meeting with the press, Adityanath said he had directed the forest department to set up an electrified fence around the nearby forest – but declined to mention who would pay for the fence, or pick up the monthly electricity bill.

Cheques delivered, Adityanath flew back to his fortified residence in the state capital of Lucknow, but the maneater remained – venturing out at night to slay the occasional buffalo and drag it back to his hideout in the tall fields of sugar cane.

I first heard of this spate of tiger-related killings in Pilibhit in the *Times of India*. FOR COMPENSATION, ELDERLY SENT TO FORESTS AS TIGER PREY, ran one startling headline. The accompanying news report claimed that villagers were sending older members of their families into the forest as tiger prey in order to collect the sorts of cheques Adityanath had been handing out.

The elders 'were willing participants in the whole affair', the article claimed, sacrificing themselves for their children to exploit the government scheme offering compensation to those killed outside Pilibhit's newly created tiger sanctuary. Those killed inside the forest were ineligible for compensation, the article noted, so the bodies needed to be relocated once the tiger had done the needful.

As evidence, the reporter offered the case of a 55-year-old woman whose adult children claimed she was ambushed by a tiger as she transplanted paddy seedlings in her fields. Her bloodstained clothes were found a kilometre and a half inside the forest.

The story was short, sensational and resonant with the cadences of Indic folklore that juxtaposed the selflessness of the aged with the grasping greed of their good-for-nothing children, along with a particular modern anxiety, as the dearth of employment has forced many Indians to live off the dwindling pensions of their parents.

'This is so pathetic! We used to hear fairy tales in our childhood days, one member of the family being sent to be eaten by the lion every day', an aggrieved reader wrote to the comments section of the *Times* website. 'Now this has come as reality. We can imagine how cruel the conditions are for the poor families, that they sacrifice their elders for feeding.'

In Pilibhit, the man tasked with keeping the press abreast of the quest to capture the maneater was a portly, bespectacled forest ranger named Satyendra Chaudhary. I found Chaudhary at the district forest office, seated behind a bare wooden desk and under a photoshopped image of Abdul Kalam – the former president and 'father' of India's nuclear weapons programme – smiling beatifically as he watered an unnaturally tall sapling.

The public works department was building a railway overbridge right through the district forest office. Rangers and clerks went on with their daily business of signing files, preparing reports and planning how to protect the forests from destruction, while around them labourers felled trees, masons demolished walls, welders sprayed luminous showers of incandescent sparks and a massive hydraulic drill dug deep holes into which massive concrete pylons would eventually be planted, its dull thudding sound regularly interrupting our conversation.

As I walked in, Chaudhary's phone buzzed with news of a fresh tiger attack. He waved me to a seat as he noted down the details on the back of an envelope: the victim was injured but not fatally, and was recovering in the district hospital. It was not clear if the offending animal was a tiger or a leopard.

'The forest is the tiger's bedroom,' said Chaudhary, tut-tutting to himself as he hung up. 'What if you walked into my bedroom without prior warning? I'd grab your collar, maybe I'd slap you. It's the same with the tiger. But if he slaps you, it will end very badly for you, Mr Aman.'

The tiger was not the problem, Chaudhary said, the people were. Years of government largesse, he claimed, had fostered a culture of dependency.

'The mentality of our people is: I will not take responsibility for my safety. I will place all my hopes in the government.'

Pilibhit's tigers were not maneaters, Chaudhary said. Most of the killings had occurred when people chanced upon a tigress and her cubs, or a tiger eating his prey. The department had issued precautions, but people were not listening.

He walked me through them: 'Number one. Do not plant sugar cane near the edges of the forest. Always farm in large groups. Stand upright so the tiger doesn't mistake you for a four-legged beast. Make lots of noise. Sing if you feel like. Shout. Clap your hands.'

I had to admit that while driving through the countryside, I had encountered no large groups of singing, clapping, upright peasants. I had, on the other hand, seen large fields of sugar cane growing right up to the trees. These fields provide perfect cover for tigers. For tigresses, the fields offer a safe haven to raise their cubs.

'A farmer will say, "It is my land, I will grow what I want."' Chaudhary shook his head again. 'Our mentality is such that we look at everything through entitlement, not through obligations.'

The tiger in Himkarpur, Chaudhary said, had spent twenty-two days moving through sugar-cane fields before he was finally spotted. There was so much cane, most of it eight feet tall, that he never had to break cover.

Tigers entered the Indian subcontinent 10,000 years ago, where they by all accounts thrived. That changed 700 years ago when the expansion of agriculture under the Mughal Empire first fragmented India's forests and split the tigers into what was to become two genetically distinct groups. The next major change, according to a study by Sandeep Sharma for the Royal Society, occurred about 200 years ago, when the colonial thirst for timber and lands for agriculture led to extensive deforestation and tiger-hunting. Yet the severest decline occurred in the past century when there was a fifty-fold decline in the Indian tiger population.

According to India's National Tiger Conservation Authority, in 2014 there were only 2,226 wild tigers left in India. Saving them from extinction has been a stated priority of the Indian government ever since the Project Tiger conservation programme was launched in 1973. Most of the tigers in India live in small pockets of land like the Pilibhit Tiger Reserve. These reserves are supposed to be linked to each other through what ecologists call 'forest corridors' – essentially wooded stretches of land that allow tigers to move from one sanctuary to another without straying into human territory – but these corridors have proved hard to protect from encroachment.

The sanctuary in Pilibhit, a horseshoe-shaped patch of forest about 700 square kilometres in area, was set up in 2014 in Uttar Pradesh, India's most populous state. Here 200 million people – roughly the population of Brazil – are crammed into an area the size of the United Kingdom.

The forest lies north-west of the Pilibhit district headquarters – a small town of about 150,000 residents, with narrow lanes choked with cars, motorcycles and electric rickshaws. There is a railway station, a crowded bazaar, a couple of hotels and an arterial avenue that leads from the bus stand past the district courts and the colonial-style bungalows of the district collector and superintendent of police into the tiger reserve. The surrounding land is flat and fertile, latticed with streams and canals built in the 1920s, and lush with paddy fields, sugar cane and a local variety of elephant grass.

The jungle in Pilibhit was managed as a commercial enterprise by the forest department for almost a century: tigers, leopards, deer, bears and monkeys shared the space with private contractors harvesting timber and bamboo, fish from the ponds and honey. The people living in the 300 villages on the periphery visited the forest several times a day to graze cattle, forage for firewood and gather a delicious wild mushroom called *kattaruvah*. Many of these villages were probably first settled by the district administration to provide a steady supply of labour for forestry work. One of the oldest settlements, for instance, is a village called Bankati – which literally means 'forest-cutting' in Hindi. When the forest was designated a tiger sanctuary in 2014, the local administration was tasked with transforming a bustling site of commerce into a wild, natural, self-regulating ecosystem sealed off from human interference. Villagers were forbidden from entering the jungle and promised jobs in tourism instead, along with cooking gas to compensate for the loss of firewood and toilets to save them the trouble of going into the forest each morning. In village meetings, forest officials promised to fence the tiger reserve to protect villagers and their cattle. None of this materialised. The villagers kept using the forest as they always had, and the new forest guards took to demanding bribes from anyone they caught. One thing did change, however: the villagers slipping into the forest no longer moved in large groups as they once did, but in ones and twos to avoid the guards. This made them vulnerable to tiger attacks.

The tigers, in the meantime, thrived in their new sanctuary. Their numbers almost doubled from about twenty-eight in 2014 to fifty in 2016, an official told me. The reserve was now teeming with tigers.

An increase in tiger attacks followed and whenever a villager was killed in the forest, panicked relatives would bring out the body to avoid prosecution for trespassing, and to perform their last rites. Government compensation was an afterthought. This ferrying around of corpses provided the fodder for the story I had read in the *Times*.

On 1 July 2017, at a little past noon, Nanki Devi brought lunch to the fields where her sons Daya Shankar Prasad, Somprakash and Dharmendar were transplanting paddy on their half-acre plot of land. The field is a rectangular wedge that juts into the eastern flank of the Pilibhit Tiger Reserve. A solitary strand of metal wire strung through three waist-high poles marks the boundary between the ordered furrows of paddy and the unruly forest beyond.

That fateful day, Prasad and his brothers were fanned out across their field when a tigress sauntered from the trees, grabbed their mother by the throat and dragged her into the forest. The men jumped onto an idling tractor and gave chase. A kilometre into the forest, they found Nanki Devi stretched out on the loamy soil, the tigress and two cubs feasting on her right leg. The men shouted. The tigers fled, though one cub tore off her leg before leaving, running away with the limb clamped between its jaws. The men retrieved Nanki Devi's corpse, laid her out in a clearing by their fields and sat waiting for the officers of the forest department. But when the officers arrived, they were quick to note that rags from Nanki's bloodied clothes were still in the forest. No compensation was paid.

A few days later, a reporter from the *Times of India* visited Nanki Devi's home, asked a few innocuous questions and spun the now notorious tale of the old people and the forest. When I arrived at Prasad's door three months later, he was still seething. The article had portrayed him as a heartless monster, he said. The local press had camped outside his home for days after it was published. 'I told the reporters, if you think I would kill my mother for compensation, I will give you double the amount,' Prasad said. 'Let me throttle your parents. Will you accept it?'

Prasad said the forest department had deliberately planted the story to deflect attention away from their inability to manage the tigers in their reserve. His mother hadn't died in a chance encounter with a wild beast, Prasad insisted. The tigers of Pilibhit had taken to hunting humans.

There isn't much academic work on why tigers become maneaters, but accepted wisdom suggests such tigers are either injured or too old to hunt. Prasad, however, had a theory of his own. 'There are two types of tigers in this forest,' he told me. 'The old ones that have always lived here and never harmed anyone, and the new tigers that kill humans. My mother was killed by a new tiger brought here by the government.'

The new tigers, Prasad said, were imported from zoos to populate the Pilibhit Tiger Reserve. 'A zoo is like a prison. These are prison tigers. You know what prison is like? You go in for one crime, and the government puts another ten crimes on you. An innocent man becomes a murderer in prison; that is what has happened to these tigers – they've become murderers, maneaters.'

Why would the government do that?

'Because once they made the tiger reserve they had to have enough tigers, no?'

But why would they make a tiger reserve if they didn't have enough tigers in the first place?

'For money. In this country, there is money behind every decision. You are in the press – you should investigate this.'

I did. Numerous government officials told me that no new tigers had been introduced into Pilibhit. 'We have the opposite problem, there are too many tigers in Pilibhit,' said Dr Utkarsh Shukla, deputy director of the Lucknow Zoo, who had spent ten fruitless days tracking the maneater in Himkarpur.

The reserve, he said, was a victim of its own success. A full-grown male Bengal tiger can command a territory of one hundred square kilometres, while a breeding female tiger needs thirty. Pilibhit Tiger Reserve is only 730 square kilometres. The forest was bursting with big cats.

'Sixteen cubs were born in Pilibhit between 2014 and 2016,' Shukla said. Tigresses usually nurse their cubs for at least two years, so this was the moment when some of these subadults would separate from their mother and compete with older tigers for prey and territory. Some would carve out their own piece of the jungle, others would slip into the sugar-cane fields surrounding the forests and bide their time. These were probably the animals the villagers described as 'zoo tigers'.

'In my experience, tiger attacks come in waves as a batch of cubs mature and are pushed out into fields where they encounter humans,' Dr Shukla said. 'We are in the middle of one such wave.'

Yet the idea of the government introducing tigers into a forest isn't as crazy as it sounds, particularly because it has been done in the past. When the Sariska Tiger Reserve in Rajasthan lost all its tigers to poaching and encroachments in 2004, for instance, the government responded by reintroducing three male and three female tigers from a nearby reserve in Ranthambore. No tigers had been relocated to Pilibhit, but perhaps the news of the Sariska relocation had found its way to Nanki Devi's village on the fringes of the forest and led villagers to distinguish between the wild tigers of the forest who kept to themselves and the apocryphal zoo tigers who had learned the murderous ways of men.

The image of the zoo tiger has stayed with me long after leaving Pilibhit. Is the myth a consequence of an inability to understand the autonomy of a creature untamed by the law? Is this what is meant by the term 'wild': to be free in a way we once cherished and have now surrendered? Perhaps the only way to survive a psychic encounter with such raw wildness is to imagine its antithesis: the zoo tiger.

On 15 July, two weeks after Nanki Devi's death, a young male tiger walked out of the forest not far from Prasad's fields, strolled through the neighbouring village of Mewatpur, terrifying all in his path, and disappeared into a large copse of sugar cane.

'It was one of the new tigers – the zoo tigers,' said Sushil Kumar, who lives along Mewatpur's main road. 'The man-eating ones.' It was slowly becoming clear to me that Kumar and Prasad spoke of the zoo tiger in much the way one would speak of a neighbour with political connections who, with a change of government, had gone from an equal to someone with the state machinery at his beck and call. The mythical zoo tiger possessed the state's most prized power – to kill without the fear of reprisal.

A few hours after the tiger was spotted in Mewatpur, the police appeared with two elephants and a forest department team followed, armed with tranquilliser guns. A unit from the Provincial Armed Constabulary showed up as well to keep the gathering crowd at bay. 'They spent a few hours roaming around the fields, but the tiger was nowhere to be seen,' said Kumar. Meanwhile, the crowd had grown to about 5,000 increasingly restive villagers.

Mewatpur's residents were of course out in full force: in February, a tiger had killed a middle-aged woman in her fields and dragged her into the forest in much the same circumstances as Nanki Devi. Here too, no compensation was paid. Villagers from nearby Shivpuriya and Rampura were there as well – they had lost three people. The crowd was furious with the government officials for denying them any compensation, for not stopping the killings, for not building the electrified fence around the sanctuary they had been promised, but most of all, they were angry because they could not believe that a department that exercised so much power over their daily lives could have no power over a wild animal.

'The forest department said: "The tiger's our national animal," ' one man recalled. 'We said, "Then give the tigers the right to vote; let them form the government." If they love the tiger so much, they should keep it in their homes. Why is it in our village?'

Tensions were high. A few months previously, a tiger had killed a teenage boy in Rampura. When grieving residents had demonstrated against the government, a forest ranger fired his weapon into the air to disperse the crowd, who attacked in retaliation. The police thrashed the people with batons, and the district administration filed criminal charges against the protesters. The locals were incensed. 'Their tiger killed our man. Their ranger fired at us, their police thrashed us and finally they filed a case against our people,' Kumar said.

That day in Mewatpur, the afternoon turned to evening with the tiger still in hiding. The crowd and the police prepared for yet another confrontation. 'Everyone wanted the tiger caught,' Kumar said, 'but when the forest department did nothing, everyone started getting angry.'

The police and the crowd exchanged blows until darkness fell and the search was called off. The tiger was momentarily forgotten as the two groups clashed.

A day after the tiger appeared in Mewatpur, trackers from the forest department found his pugmarks four kilometres west, in the village of Tahapauta. A week later he killed and ate a nilgai antelope in Tandola. Three days later, the *Times* reported that the tiger was spotted less than 250 yards from the Pilibhit courthouse, prompting the district judge to take serious cognisance of the matter and direct the forest department to 'ensure tigers do not come near the court in the future'. Department records show that he killed five more animals over the next ten days.

Twenty days after he left the forest, he was finally cornered again in Pinjara village, about twenty kilometres as the crow flies from Mewatpur. Once more a large crowd gathered on the edges of the field, but the animal stayed put. The search was called off at dusk and everyone was instructed to go home as it was too dangerous to be around a cornered, frightened tiger in the dark.

Two days later, at seven in the morning, the tiger killed Tasleem Ahmed as he was hunched over in his field in the village of Adauli. Villagers were still agog with excitement when I visited a month later. 'An incredible scene. Ten thousand people gathered,' Margu Hussain Salmani recounted at a tea shop just outside the village. 'People were getting off buses, running straight towards the village, saying, "Where's the tiger? Where's the tiger?" '

In Adauli, the presence of the tiger provoked both terror and exhilaration. Onlookers would cast a cursory, respectful glance at Tasleem's corpse, but it was the tiger they really wanted to see. 'Everyone had seen a dead body, but none of us had ever seen a tiger before.'

When a team from the forest department was finally allowed through the crowd, they found the tiger perched on the low boughs of a mango tree. Dusk was nigh. A veterinarian from the forest department aimed his tranquilliser gun, fired a dart and struck the tiger on its rump. The startled tiger leapt off the tree, bolted into the nearest sugar-cane field and vanished from sight. 'The tranquilliser didn't work,' said Salmani. 'I don't think it even hit the tiger. Few departments are as useless as our forest department.'

'The howling crowd ran straight at the tiger,' said forest ranger Anil Shah, who was there when it happened. 'All these people know how to do is howl.'

165

A tranquilliser usually takes between ten and fifteen minutes to act, Dr Shukla later told me, but it can take longer if the animal is stressed and feels it is in immediate danger. The tiger in Adauli would have been stressed, the crowd howling and chasing after it. It must have crashed deliriously through the twilit cane fields, finally buckling under the powerful sedative and falling over senseless.

The next morning it woke up and killed Shamsur Rehman as he weeded his fields in the neighbouring village, eating most of his body from the waist down. It slipped away again when Rehman's friends came looking for him. 'I can still see the expression on his face,' said Mohammed Shamshad, Rehman's brother-in-law. 'His face was frozen in fear. It was a fear like I have never seen before.'

The crowds formed again in protest. This time, they won a minor victory against the local government. They held district officials hostage until they all signed an undertaking hastily scrawled on a sheet of paper torn from a child's notebook:

> Today, on 8/8/17, at 11.00 a.m., village Serenda Patti, resident Shamsur Rehman, son of Abdul Rehman, was preyed on by a tiger. His corpse was found in his fields. On account of this misfortune, he will receive Rs 30,000 from the district administration, Rs 5 lac from life insurance, and Rs 5 lac from the forest department.

The forest department paid Rehman his compensation, but a relative told me they were still figuring out if he had any life insurance at all. 'The officials were terrified that the crowd would thrash them, so they just wrote something to keep the crowd calm,' said Shamshad.

The tiger struck again two days later in Himkarpur, snapping Kunvar Singh's neck with a quick blow to the throat. The tiger was dragging Singh away when his sons grabbed their father's corpse's legs and pulled him back. With three deaths in four days, the forest department finally got its act together. They were going on the hunt.

Hunting tigers is a long-established way for rulers to impress their subjects; a way to illustrate the expanse of their authority by directing it against a beast that in its essence is fearsome and ungovernable. In the cane fields of Pilibhit, I wondered what the forest department's hapless quest to tranquillise the maneater could tell us about the modern Indian state and its subjects. As ever, I turned to Chaudhary, the ranger.

'Think of the tiger as a dacoit, a bandit, Mr Aman,' Chaudhary told me over the phone. 'It is easy to shoot a dacoit, much harder to capture him alive, and hardest to turn the dacoit into a saint.'

Once tranquillised, the tiger would most likely be sent to serve out a life sentence at the Lucknow Zoo, Chaudhary said. 'There is a very small chance he could be sent back to the jungle.' The modern state does not take lives unless pushed to do so. Rather it expends much energy to survey, enumerate, incarcerate, compensate and, if possible, rehabilitate its subjects.

To capture the maneater of Pilibhit, the forest department erected three tall watchtowers, or *machchans*, at the corners of a five-square-kilometre patch of sugar cane on the banks of the Deva River. They strung up twenty-two nets and installed twenty cameras. They placed meat in three cages, booby-trapped to swing shut when the tiger entered. A fourth covered cage was kept ready to transfer the captured tiger from the village to the district headquarters. They flew five drones, including one with a thermal camera, over the field. And in a distinctly Mughal touch, four trained elephants – Gangakali, Pawankali, Gajraj and Batalik – stood by to get vets as close to the tiger as possible. Finally, a live buffalo calf was tethered just outside the fields as a lure.

'You localise the animal. Then, offer it prey to keep it from eating more humans,' Dr Shukla told me, explaining their strategy. 'Then, you wait for it to relax and show itself and you tranquillise it.'

Guidelines published by the National Tiger Conservation Authority distinguish between tigers that have killed humans by accident and those that actively stalk and hunt humans as prey. Once a tiger has been positively identified as a maneater, the NTCA guidelines state that all attempts should be made to capture the tiger and relocate it to a zoo, failing which it should be killed in accordance with a rigorous protocol to avoid killing the wrong animal by accident.

The guidelines mandate that a tiger can only be tranquillised between dawn and dusk, so Dr Shukla spent two weeks waiting for the tiger to approach the live bait during the day, but the tiger only struck at night. 'Darting has to be in the daytime,' Dr Shukla said. 'The last thing you want is a half-drugged tiger stumbling into the river at night and drowning.'

The villagers I spoke with noted that the sensitivity shown to the tiger by the administration was completely absent in their interactions with its victims. 'At night, a guard can see the tiger killing the buffalo, but he can't dart it,' said Nirmal Lal Maurya, the headman of Pinjara village. 'When we ask the guard, he says, "If the tiger drowns I'll lose my job." But if the tiger kills another man, no one will lose their job.'

From 10 August, the day of its last human kill, until 11 September, the tiger ate five buffalo and two sheep. 'The sixth buffalo was a bit skittish,' said a forest tracker. 'One night she broke her rope and ran off towards the river. The tiger ran after her.'

The next day the buffalo was found tied up in a shed in Pinjara village. The tiger, in the meantime, was nowhere to be found. 'The tiger has left Himkarpur,' ranger Chaudhary told me. 'We haven't seen any pugmarks since 11 September, our cameras haven't captured any photos.'

But no one in Himkarpur believed his department. 'They've fed the tiger so much, why would it ever leave?' said Nirmal Lal Maurya. 'Now they've stopped feeding him. He's going to kill someone soon.'

Shortly before I left Pilibhit, I stopped by the home of Shamsur Rehman, the second person the tiger killed and partially ate. At his modest mud-and-brick house, Shamshad, his brother-in-law, offered to take me to the spot where they found Rehman's corpse.

We jumped onto a motorcycle and rode as far into the fields as the bike would go, after which we proceeded on foot through mango orchards, knee-high paddy and the omnipresent sugar cane, haunted by wild tigers and the spirits of those they had eaten.

Twilight was upon us and the shadows grew longer; the boundaries between field, orchard and forest blurred. I noticed that Shamshad was breathing in long gasps that grew more laboured as we spotted a broken pair of green rubber slippers, a pair of torn black pants and a ripped cotton undershirt. 'These are his, these are his', Shamshad said. He was sobbing now. 'Why are they still here, why are they still here? I can still see him. There was just his torso, everything else was eaten away. I can still see his frozen face. Never have I seen a fear like that.'

'Would it have felt different if he had fallen off a motorcycle?' I asked.

Shamshad was quiet for a long time. 'It ate him,' he said. 'That's what I can't unsee. It ate him.'

The wind picked up, the cane rustled. A monkey screamed in a mango tree.

I realised that Shamshad and I were out by ourselves at night with a maneater on the prowl. Was it a kinship of species that Shamshad and I shared then: two humans on the edge of a forest contemplating a lurking predator? Did a part of Shamshad secretly wish that the tiger would continue to elude the forest department and quietly live out his life in the forest, like I did? Could some deaths be mourned, but not avenged?

As we made our way back to the village I remembered Ranger Chaudhary's precautions: I clapped my hands and Shamshad made a loud 'ha-ha-ha' sound that carried across the lonely fields. ∎

GIORGIO SOMMER
Cast of a Dog Killed by the Eruption of Mount Vesuvius, Pompeii, c.1874
© THE J PAUL GETTY MUSEUM

DOG

Nadeem Aslam

More than once the new dog was aggressive, a stab of fire, but I did not tell the grown-ups. I feared they would take him away. I was ten years old, and I pretended that the scratches and marks on my skin were caused by a thorn bush or by a fall.

He was from the hills. In the 1960s a dam was constructed in northern Pakistan, submerging hundreds of villages, a number of towns and many tracts of forestland. Some of the displaced people arrived to live on the outskirts of the city where I grew up. From this refugee camp, a sixteen-year-old girl named Iqbal came to work in our neighbours' house. She told me about her village in the hills, how it now lay underwater with the minarets of the mosque sticking out, the herons perching on the tips. Already at that age, books had become a habit and therefore a need for me. During the long afternoons, when the rest of the family slept, I would make my way surreptitiously to the roof and find a place to read. Iqbal would appear from the next roof and join me. She was addicted to nasvaar – a narcotic powder made with green tobacco and slaked lime. I now know that in 1561 the French ambassador in Portugal had sent nasvaar to Catherine de' Medici, as a cure for her son's constant migraines. Iqbal would take out the pungent green stuff – she carried it in a twist of cellophane hidden in the waistband of her trousers – and place it under her lower lip and lie down beside me on the floor, her eyes closed. Her employers had suspected her of using nasvaar, but she had not only denied it, she had sworn on the Quran to placate them. She had been hired to look after small children and the fear was that she would feed it to them, to make them docile, less demanding. And so both of us hid on the roof during those searingly hot afternoons: I would read, and she dozed beside me, sometimes wordlessly, sometimes speaking in a low murmur about various things, including her lost village.

Occasionally she went back to visit family members who had managed to remain in the hills. Once she returned with the gift of a deer antler for me, and later there were several interesting pebbles, the skull of a bird with a red beak, large map-like moth wings and strange scaled fruit that at first made me think they were pangolin eggs. When I was ten she brought a puppy. From the folds of her shawl it sniffed the air, each whisker as nervous as a compass needle. We were soon inseparable. In certain lights there was a strange glow to him, an intense brilliance in his eyes that I hadn't encountered in any other dog. I had been reading about 'candle-birds', whose flesh was so enriched with oil that a bird could be threaded whole onto a wick and burned as a source of light. My dog grew fast and was deeply affectionate on the whole, but there were those brief moments of anger, something electric spilling into the air from him, his teeth bare with hate for me or for what I represented.

One day a blind beggar stopped chewing for a few moments when the dog walked past.

On another occasion a horse looked at him for a long time and then suddenly reared up, having understood something.

The knock on the door came at midnight, waking the entire household. It was our neighbours – Iqbal's employers – and Iqbal was with them, as were her parents.

They revealed that the dog was in fact a wolf cub.

His identity had become blurred as he passed from hand to hand in the hills, after the forest he had lived in had been submerged, separating him from his mother and the rest of the pack. That strange light I had noticed in his eyes – it had been him searching for a mirror in which to see himself.

No one could give me a precise answer as to what happened to him after he was taken away that night. I kept asking with urgency and desperation, but after a while I understood that I must stop. Iqbal was caught with nasvaar on her person one day and let go by our neighbours. In another few months the refugee camp where she had lived was declared illegal by the authorities and demolished, and she and her family were forced to move on. I never saw her again. She and the dog and the handful of facts associated with them became a kind of ache I can still feel inside me, a sense of defeat and loss. I had taught him to roll over, and I see it now in my mind's eye: for a fraction of a second – with his legs in the air and his head twisting – he resembles his cousin from Pompeii. ■

S peedy came already named from the Isle of Wight RSPCA. She was the runt; she looked like a white-and-brown goose. She tucked her beak into the crook of my arm as we drove home.

Mine.

The first time she caught a squirrel in the park, decapitated it, swallowed the thick middle, crunched the legs, all that was left was the tail and head, like a key ring.

The hive of baby rabbits she dug up – she consumed the lot, blind squeaking babies, as simply as I ate peanuts.

The worst, her cannibal heart, she killed a fox cub, snapped its neck and ploughed into its belly like watermelon.

Speedy wanted to swallow the world.

She was not like our other dogs who would occasionally appear at the caravan door, requiring their myxomatosis rabbits cooked. The brutal part was large – she was more dog than the others, didn't think of herself as human, didn't think of herself at all – she was a shark encountering life through bite. But she was mine, she belonged to me, and she wanted to smell the stickleback at the bottom of my net, bounce with me like an Arctic fox in the long grass, circle me at speed like a spring mechanism had tripped within her, her face turning loopy and daft, her body not running, but opening and closing.

My fingers knew every inch of her; I would fossick out the thorns in her head, the seeds from between her toes, the ticks from her ears. Visits to the vet because of accidents were common. She took a corner too sharply and left a hank of her skin hanging there on a metal fence like a torn sock. She chased a squirrel into a mountain bike and shattered her shoulder blade, became part machine with a metal plate in there. Slit her undercarriage on barbed wire chasing sheep. Had part of her nose pulled off by a red squirrel.

Then the last visit, when she was old and scared, my fingertips grasping for memory, the feel of her warty cheek, her ears, cold velvet. And her throat soft, even in old age immaculate, the underbelly of a shark. The vet stopped her heart as she blindly wolfed biscuits from my hand, and I felt in the broken-down sadness of loss that he could have given her just a moment more to finish the handful, that she had not quite succeeded in her quest to swallow everything. ∎

WINTERKILL

Cal Flyn

When we reach the bothy they are already there, watching us from high on the crags overlooking the water. When we crossed the loch, outboard motor thrumming, we crossed over into their domain, and now the hills are thick with their bodies.

We've barely arrived – still tasting the chill, stale air of the empty house, staking claims on stained mattresses – when Julien's attention is caught by something seen through the back-room window, a warped pane rimmed with dust and the breath of previous occupants. 'They're up there now,' he says simply. 'Let's go.'

Outside is all sky: indigo ink seeping in from the east. There is just time. Within minutes we are out the door and shinning up the hill face without speaking, gaining height fast. The wind is whipping up, moving in great currents over the ridge. It comes in waves, smashing against us and then withdrawing, dragging the air from our lungs as it does. I open my collar and let cold air creep over hot flesh.

Julien and Storm are way out in front, goat-footed over tussocks and hags. I try to match their pace – copying how, each time they round a false summit, they drop low to the ground and creep through the heather on elbows, pressing their abdomens into the mud, all the time scanning the hillside for movement.

After a while they slow to a stop and we bunch up together. Storm catches my eye and points hammily beyond the boulder he is using as a windbreak. I nod, coming to rest at his feet, sinking my hands into long dead grass as if it were hair. I wait a beat, then lift my head, bringing my eyes above the stone parapet.

We are close enough to see the face in detail: her domed, almost Roman, profile, which she tosses about as dark eyes flash in every direction. Suspicious: not good. The breeze is turbulent, changeable. We'd tried to keep it in our faces, but it's begun to swing wildly around; perhaps she caught a noseful of us – just for one terrifying moment – and is now working out in which direction to run.

I try to drop my head imperceptibly back down behind the rock. When I muster the courage to look again, the face has gone.

Up ahead, Julien cranes forward from his foxhole then stands up, shaking his head, face distressed. Gone.

We start picking our way east, towards the burn, so we can trace its path back to the house. It bubbles and froths merrily, all the time slicing down into the hillside like a bandsaw: cutting a steep, narrow gorge of black wet spatter rock that tumbles down precipitously ahead of us.

And then, there they are. Two females and a juvenile on the opposite bank, standing like phantoms in the gloaming. They haven't seen us. I am struck silent. Julien twists around, pale face a ghostly glimmer, and gestures to Adrian: *come*. Adrian goes, army-crawling across wet earth. They disappear beneath a precipice leaving the three of us to wait in silence.

A minute passes, then another. I lie back against the heather, thinking no particular thoughts. A shot rings out, impossibly loud.

A moment of confusion. The gully is deserted. I sit up stupidly, feeling suddenly alone, and forlorn. Then Adrian and Julien appear again on the ledge below, waving us down. They got one: a crack shot, right through the spine. Dropped straight from the rock face into the water. She's dead.

It is 13 February, and Julien and Storm have been doing this all winter long. This hind (an older specimen, unusually large, very lean and – as it transpires later, when we split her open and spill her guts on the ground – several months pregnant) is their twenty-first kill of the season.

But it's not enough. Julien has a target he must hit: thirty animals – or 'beasts', as he calls them, a strange word from his French mouth – and very little time left in which to meet it. In Scotland, the hind-shooting season closes at dusk on the fifteenth. Until then here we are, five of us – four men and one woman: me – spending our days stalking deer and our nights in an empty house, with a fireplace at each end and little else. No electricity, no running water. We eat stew from a scorched iron pot over the fire, drink water from the peaty burn that runs by the gable end. Hanging from two nails by the door is a shovel that comprises the toilet.

A doorless lean-to slouches heavily against the back wall. It is here we take the dead deer for hanging. Julien throws a karabiner attached to a length of rope over a rafter and lowers it down, scattering bird droppings and cobwebs upon us as he does. Threading the cord through two slits cut in her hocks, he clips rope to rope and hoists her like a flag.

I watch her ascent with the same clouded mix of curiosity and disquiet as earlier I regarded that lifeless fawn lying limp in its amniotic shroud upon the heather. What was animal is now object; it is a truth both terrible and prosaic. I observe my reactions as if from above, lifting and weighing each thought as it comes to me, alert for squeamishness. There is some. But not as much, perhaps, as I expected.

Julien bends over her rent chest, headlamp illuminating the torso from within, and sets to work again with his knife and a surgeon's manner. It is easy to trace the path of the bullet: its entry and exit, the single shattered vertebra between. A tragedy in one act. The rest is more complicated. When he's done, he dashes a bucket of water into the space where her vital organs were. I watch, taking my cues from those who have done this before. Gore drips on the hard-packed floor.

Then we slide her down the length of the rafter, drawing her like a curtain, to make room for the rest.

No one owns the red deer. But if you own the land that they live on – graze from, shelter in, pass through – then you assume responsibility for their management. In Scotland, where their numbers have doubled in the last fifty years, such stewardship has come to mean one thing: the annual cull.

And it is in the Highlands where the country's deer problem is clear to be seen: they gorge themselves upon gardens and crops and vegetable patches, they run blindly into the road as speeding cars approach. The biggest issue is that of overgrazing, which affects huge swathes of the country, including a large number of sites recognised by the government to be of special scientific interest or ecological importance.

The true scale of the problem is hard to gauge, but our best guess is that there might now be as many as 1.5 million deer in the UK, at least half of them in Scotland; more than at any time since the last Ice Age. They roam bare hills in vast herds – in the Cairngorms they have been seen in herds a thousand animals strong, steam rising from their massed ranks. They swarm over the fells like a plague in Moses' Egypt, covering the land like a cloak, picking it clean, moving off as fast as they arrived.

And with the deer comes plague of another sort: cases of Lyme disease, spread by ticks that use the deer as hosts, have rocketed – in some areas reaching epidemic proportions. But perhaps the most pressing concerns are environmental ones. The red deer eat and eat, overwhelming a delicate moorland ecosystem, trampling the ground, shearing the hillside of vegetation and stripping the bark from the trees.

In Glen Affric, for example, volunteers from the charity Trees for Life spent many weeks planting native trees in the stark western reaches of the glen. They hoped to build a forest corridor from east to west coasts, joining up the fragments of the remaining Caledonian Forest. But when the organisation's founder Alan Featherstone returned to the site in 2015, he found their sturdy deer fences flattened by winter snowdrifts, and the saplings inside (birches, willows, rowans) bitten hard back. More than a decade's growth had been undone in a matter of weeks.

Now, until the fences are rebuilt, the shorn stems will struggle to grow: new shoots and leaves nipped off as fast as they appear, their progress arrested indefinitely.

The ascendance of the deer is attributed in large part to the disappearance of the largest carnivores from the British Isles: wolves. The last grey wolf was killed in 1860, and since then cervids have roamed the country unfettered by predators. Undisturbed, a herd of 300 has the potential to grow to 3,000 in the space of thirteen years. So the role of the predator, the role of the wolf, is what the estate owners of Scotland now cast themselves in.

Around 100,000 deer are killed in Scotland every year, the vast majority of them red deer. Some are killed on traditional sporting estates, where for generations southerners and City types have flooded, keen to shoot a monarch of the glen. But fewer dream of shooting the hinds, the real way to impact upon population growth, and so the responsibility falls to the owners.

Perhaps perversely, it is the conservation lobby who are the most vociferous proponents of the culls. Those concerned with woodland and wild flowers argue for an all-out war, pointing to research from the University of East Anglia which mooted a mass cull of 50–60 per cent of all deer. Wildlife foundations find themselves calling for the deaths of tens of thousands of wild animals.

The prospect of mass shooting is one that arouses great passion; even if arguments come forth from unexpected quarters. If the environmentalists are mounting a war, the shooting estates – those professional deer killers – call for peace, for the gentle approach.

They fear the culls will go too far; that something special will be lost.

Twice-yearly, landowners in each region meet in 'deer management groups' to share their targets for the year. The collective approach is necessary, as the deer drift back and forth across the heather moor in tides aligned with the seasons. They cross boundaries between estates on open hillsides, unmarked by fences or walls. In this way, each landowner's actions impact directly upon his neighbours: if one shirks his duty in the annual cull, numbers across the whole region rebound – the dilemma of the commons.

It is in their interests to cooperate, then, but with so many clashing views and beliefs, these so-called management groups often grow unmanageable.

Julien, my friend with the rifle, has been in charge of deer management on the East Rhidorroch Estate near Ullapool for the last three years. Having come as a backpacker, looking to work in exchange for accommodation and experience, he fell in love with Iona, the middle daughter of the owners, and together the young couple took over the running of the remote estate.

At first a neighbour held the stalking rights – and cull responsibilities – but when the lease came up, it seemed natural that they should reclaim them. For Julien, who studied ecology at university, it was an interesting way of applying the theory. And it was all around them, here in the west Highlands, where the hinds and many-pointed stags roamed the hills in their bands; ghillies coming by on their quad bikes in bloodstained tweeds. This was part of the culture of his adopted home, and wasn't it one reason he'd found this place so enchanting?

Inevitably, the reality turned out to be rather complicated; the responsibility of the cull onerous for an inexperienced Frenchman who had never before owned a gun. Highland ghillies are often born of stalking families, have spent their whole lives on the hill. They know the ways of the deer, the way they move, the way they think. They have breathed in that musk, that thick throaty scent of the animal that never leaves you. They know how the weather affects their behaviour, where they are to be found come sunrise, come noon, come sunset.

But as hard as all of this was to learn, negotiating the politics of deer was harder. Twice a year, the couple are now expected to attend the meetings of their local deer management group – sprawling, hours-long meetings in dreary hotel conference rooms which never seem to come to a consensus.

Last time, Iona tells me, there was more than an hour of fractious back-and-forth before they even got on to the subject of deer. Then, their nearest neighbour stood up to read aloud a long list of complaints, before departing abruptly to go to church. Iona was embarrassed. 'It's the only time we ever meet some of the other owners. Although some of them send gamekeepers in their place.' The main takeaway from the meeting was that they must now contribute more money for helicopter surveys.

The sheer expense of it all has been another nasty revelation. Thousands just for the basic equipment: a £600 rifle, a £1,500 scope. A moderator to muffle the gunshot. The full outfit in heathery tones: smock, trousers, heavy-duty boots, balaclava. Training courses. And the days and days that might be spent working the sheep instead now passed in wolves' clothing on the mountain.

To begin with, Julien couldn't get it right, ruining his chances a different way every time. Walking upwind of the deer. Revealing himself on the skyline. Missing his chance as his fingers quivered on the trigger. Often he returned at dusk, empty-handed and so exhausted that at 4 p.m. he would topple into bed and stay there until the rise of the low winter sun at 10 a.m., when he would head out all over again.

Then, on one of the coldest days of the year, his efforts were rewarded. Heading out alone, camouflaged in a snow-white bodysuit, he finally attained invisibility. In a land of whiteness and silence, he became white, he became silent.

A group of seventy deer moved across the hillside and, eyes sliding past his motionless body in the snow, came to surround him. 'They were everywhere,' he recalls. 'Playing and fighting. They had no idea I was there.' He lay like a rock in their midst, sizing them up. He spotted an elderly underweight hind, a prime target, and steeled himself for action.

Seconds passed. If I shoot, he remembers thinking, this beautiful moment will be over forever. Then he pulled the trigger.

As a teenager growing up in genteel St Andrews, Mike Daniels dreamed of saving the world. He was 'hippyish', he says. Vegetarian. Keen to make his mark. When he was sixteen he organised a period of work experience at Creag Meagaidh, a nature reserve in the Cairngorms where woolly willow and saxifrage grow on a gilded mountain plateau; an enclave of dotterel and snow bunting and mountain hare.

On his first day, nervous and excited, he was picked up from the nearest station and driven to where he'd be staying, and as they got out of the car, they spotted a deer wandering in the woods nearby. Things moved quickly. The man who was driving leapt out, grabbing his rifle from the back. He shot the deer, gutted it on the side of the road, then lifted it onto the roof.

'Blood was dripping down the windscreen,' Mike says. 'That was my introduction.'

Though shocking for an idealistic teen, it was a fitting start for a career that has come to be defined by the difficult relationship between conservation and wild deer. Mike sees a similar emotional journey in many of those who have since come to work with him in the field. 'They think the deer are lovely, that Scotland is beautiful . . . and then they learn more about it.' Deer culls, he now believes – having seen the devastation they can wreak first-hand – are a necessary evil. A way of re-establishing the natural order.

Back in 2004, Mike was working for what was then called the Deer Commission when he and his colleagues were called in to conduct an emergency cull at Glenfeshie, an estate owned by a Danish billionaire in the Cairngorms National Park, where deer numbers had been allowed to grow to remarkable levels, an estimated 95 per square kilometre. Sharpshooters were flown in by helicopter to the estate's remotest corners; dozens of contract stalkers were bussed in for an intensive effort. Mike was in the larder, processing the bodies. Altogether, more than 500 deer were slaughtered that season.

The cull, the first state intervention on a private estate, created an enormous fuss. Animal rights campaigners accused the commission of acting illegally. Local gamekeepers staged a mass protest against the 'carnage', which, they said, went against 'our way of life, our morals, our beliefs . . . and above all our respect for the deer'. Neighbouring landowners and local residents took to the airwaves to voice their disapproval.

Now, as the head of land management of the John Muir Trust, a charity dedicated to the preservation of Scotland's wild places, Mike sees those same arguments playing out time and again. As the owner of several sizeable landholdings across the country, the conservation group has been using its power to manage the land in a way that prioritises the environment, specifically by preserving and regenerating fragments of the once-great Caledonian Forest.

To do so, they say, they must significantly increase the number of deer culled on their properties. The alternative – fencing off the vulnerable woodlands – is not an option. Mike sighs when I bring it up: 'the F word'. He and the trust both see fencing as treating 'the symptoms not the cause', and it keeps the deer from seeking shelter in the harsh weather of the Scottish winter. They would rather reduce numbers so significantly as to render fences unnecessary.

However sound their reasoning, it does nothing to endear them to the owners of neighbouring sporting estates. Such an estate's value is partly based on the number of stags available to shoot each year – a good rule of thumb being around one in every sixteen stags on the hill. And those who pay for the pleasure of shooting a stag (or far more, for the pleasure of owning a private deer forest) don't wish to spend too long fruitlessly roaming the glens without a sighting. But though some estates do make significant income from slaughter tourism, they are in the minority. 'It's a bit like owning a football club. A small

CAL FLYN

few – the Chelseas, the Man Uniteds – are big money-spinners. But
generally, they run at a loss.'

A Highland truism: you don't get rich from owning a deer forest;
you own a deer forest because you are rich. Either way, the John Muir
Trust's no-holds-barred tactics have made them plenty of enemies.
Sporadically a new skirmish breaks out: in Knoydart, a wild western
peninsula accessed only by boat, an argument flared up in 2015 when
the trust's stalkers shot dozens of stags more than their agreed target.
Some, shot down in the most far-flung places, were left to rot where
they fell and be picked over by the eagles.

The language employed by protesters in these cases is emotive:
those who conduct the cull are accused of 'senseless slaughter', of
creating a 'bloodbath', or a 'massacre'. To Mike, these slurs are hurtful
and hypocritical: numbers shot by the John Muir Trust are a fraction
of the total culled each year across the country. And many of those
levelling the charges are shooting deer themselves.

But the controversy speaks of a deep unease about mass killing
among many of those who earn their living on the hill. The
gamekeepers protesting at Glenfeshie were not parading their
'respect' for their quarry for effect. A specialised strand of folk ethics
has grown up among stalkers: the rules are based on perceived
sportsmanship, on fairness, on tradition. To them, flying in by
helicopter simply *feels* wrong, like cheating. So does leaving carcasses
to rot. So does taking too many in one go.

What marks a cull? What marks a massacre? Big questions, these,
to ponder as you stare down the barrel of a rifle.

My first shot comes in the early afternoon, after a long scramble
down a rocky channel in silence, ankle-deep in water. I'm a
good shot – but the trick is getting close enough to try. One hundred
metres is ideal, but on this bare, coverless expanse it seems an
impossible feat.

Now, though, the little gully has led us like a secret passageway to
the heart of the glen, where around a dozen deer are grazing. It's the

best chance we've had all day. Breathing heavily, I set up the rifle and lie down with the butt pressed flush to my shoulder.

On Julien's orders, taking the drift of wind and gravity into account, I float the cross hairs somewhere just over the shoulder of a hind who stands perfectly still, side-on, like a target in a shooting gallery. I let the breath leave my body. I fire.

The gun recoils heavily into my shoulder and I lose sight of her. The boom of gunshot ricochets off the sides of the glen, but when I turn the scope back on the hind, she remains as she was, though her jaw has stilled. Adrenaline pounds my system – did I miss her? – and my hands are shaking as I draw away from the gun, but Julien waves me back – *wait* – and I see the deer take a few tentative steps away from the herd before she quietly folds her legs underneath herself and lies down. She sounds no alarm. The deer around her continue to graze, undisturbed.

I was prepared for mass panic, a thunderous retreat. Not this. This dumb acceptance, a total lack of comprehension. My heart bleeds for them. We could take them all now if we wanted. Bang. Bang. Bang. Bang.

We won't. But we must take one more. Storm points to the bandy-legged calf that has followed my quarry to where she has fallen. We have to shoot it now too. More gamekeeper ethics: it is kinder to shoot it than leave it to starve.

Julien is watching me carefully. 'Do you want me to do it?'

I shake my head, take aim.

Later, blood glugs from an incision cut in the hind's throat, like wine from a bottle. It pours away into the peat, soaked up by the sphagnum like a sponge. When I stand, my knees are patched with claret.

Once, years ago, I watched as a cat was being spayed: the vet opening its torso like a cabinet, gloved hands dipping into negative space. It comes to mind as I kneel over the hind's body for the gutting, the 'gralloching'. There's more blood this time certainly, with no nurse to suction it away. It fills the cavity between diaphragm and pelvis, uncomfortably hot, like a sink full of dishes. I'm in it up to my elbows.

The membranes of the organs are thin and delicate, silken. Their edges are fluid, shape-shifting in my hands. But still I recognise each form as I pull them out: stomach, liver, kidneys.

I think of every time I've ever used the word 'visceral' and resolve never again to take it in vain. What did I know of viscera until I felt the chain-link of intestine running through my fingers? How dare I allude to this most intimate of acts? The touch of another creature's innards, of following the transfiguration of grass to fumet as one traces digestive tract from throat to tail. Of how, having separated rectum from anus, one might tie off the tube and hold its contents safe in a purse made of muscle.

It is late by the time we finish, our new additions now hanging in the outhouse in the dark. I take the empty bucket down to the burn to clean, and while I'm there I wash the blood from my hands, from my arms, from my face. The water is biting cold, crystal clear. It tastes better than anything I've ever drunk before.

When I return, the others have gone in to get a fire going. I step into the room to set the bucket on the floor, and as I bend down I can sense them behind me, feet to the sky, shifting with slight pendular motions. The effect is unnerving. As if I'm standing in a crowded room, and no one is speaking.

In a grassy hollow behind the white-sand beach at Achmelvich, the crofter Ray Mackay lives in a wooden house overlooking a small green lochan dappled with water lilies.

I sit at the table, admiring the view, and momentarily he arrives bearing tea and an A4 folder of grievances. He, and the Assynt Crofters' Trust, of which he is vice chair, have been fighting a bitter battle of increasingly high stakes with the government over the fate of the red deer on their land.

Their land. That's the operative term. Back in the early nineties, the Assynt crofters fought a different battle – a long one and a hard one – when they undertook the first community buyout of a private estate, raising hundreds of thousands of pounds to buy the land they lived on and worked from an absentee landlord they had wrestled with for years.

The case of the Assynt crofters came to symbolise the many inequities of land ownership in Scotland, where only 500 individuals own more than half the land, and where the pain of mass dispossession during the eighteenth and nineteenth centuries still echoes loudly in the culture and the politics. The crofters' case went right to the heart of the question of what it really means to own a place. As the poet Norman MacCaig wrote in his paean to the region, 'A Man in Assynt':

> Who possesses this landscape? —
> The man who bought it or
> I who am possessed by it?

When finally the crofters prevailed, MacCaig's question lost its bite – the land was theirs, whichever way you looked at it. Yet, more than two decades on, the question of who has ultimate control has surfaced once more.

The problem, says Ray, revolves around a remnant of old-growth woodland situated partly on their land. A governmental body, Scottish Natural Heritage, believes it to be at risk from overgrazing and has ordered them to undertake an emergency cull; the Crofters' Trust disagrees, questioning the population estimates, pointing to abnormalities in the surveys. It is not just the principle of the matter, says Ray. They shoot deer for management reasons every year. For them the issue is a matter of scale. If they accept the mass cull, they believe they could send the deer on their estate into a precipitous decline.

The crofters have worked hard to escape their debts, to make the community sustainable. 'We survived,' Ray says. 'That was not a given.' Assynt is not a wealthy area. Small crofting townships of modest whitewashed cottages and modern bungalows cling to the rugged coastline, linked by winding, single-track roads. The peninsula's interior is an undulating blanket of peat bog: sodden, stony, ill-suited to agriculture. There are more deer here than people. He shows me the latest accounts: fewer costs, income from stalking and venison sales amounts to nearly a sixth of total profits. Here the deer are an asset, not a hobby – no football team vanity project – and they do not intend to risk the depletion of this natural resource.

But now – having declined a voluntary cull – the trust faces becoming another test case. If nothing changes, this will be the first use of a section 8 order: a forced cull. The trust will be fined £40,000 and have to pay the costs of the operation – which will be sizeable. For the government it could be embarrassing: to use these legal powers for the first time against a community group once a cause célèbre and darling of the devolved parliament.

The threats are a particularly bitter pill to swallow because Scottish Natural Heritage itself donated money towards the crofters' buyout in 1993. 'Not a day passes when we don't regret taking that money.'

There is a certain class of conservationist, continues Ray, who came of age post-Rachel Carson's landmark *Silent Spring*, and trained in this new and passionate field. When they graduated, they sought jobs where they could make use of their knowledge. But most of the country is dominated by farming and industry – 'so they end up here. On the fringes.'

They are very keen, and their hearts are in the right place, he says, but at a basic, unarguable level, they are usually incomers. When they drive in, making demands, it immediately sets up a tension. 'The undercurrent is that they seem to be saying that we are not managing our environment as well as we could. But *this* is the place where you find the wild cats. The white-throated divers.'

He tells me about a map drawn up recently by the government that identified the trust's North Assynt Estate as one of the country's most extensive areas of wilderness. I nod unthinkingly in approval, picturing the grand curving aspect of the Assynt landscape, where solitary pillars of gneiss stand sentry long after their sandstone neighbours were scoured away by glaciers, themselves now long melted away. It is a stark, treeless place where golden eagles flash over a gilded, wind-scoured moonscape of moor and blanket bog.

'But these are our common grazings!' cries Ray. 'One day they decide it to be "wild land" but for us it's where we work.'

His words recall the writing of William Cronon, the environmental historian who, in 1995, wrote that 'far from being the one place on earth that stands apart from humanity, wilderness is quite profoundly a human creation'. Cronon, an American, was addressing the cult of wilderness that had grown up in his country, thanks in no small part to the work of John Muir, the Scotsman Mike's charity was named for, whose solitary writing and wandering in the Sierra Nevada inspired generations, not least those responsible for the institution of the national park system and the Wilderness Act of 1964, which sought to protect those places still 'untrammeled by man, where man himself is a visitor who does not remain'. Such a definition must have surprised those who, like the Ahwahneechees of Yosemite, had lived in these beauty spots for many centuries. The last of the Ahwahneechees were evicted from the national park, their homes razed, in 1969.

The concept of 'wilderness' then is a nebulous one; one based on aesthetics as much as on human geography. The wide-open spaces of Assynt are a case in point: to the untrained eye, it appears an untamed, untameable land. To its occupants, it is laced with human history.

Seen through this prism, the question of what is natural and what is unnatural is a tangled one. Is the proliferation of deer the result of human meddling? In all likelihood, yes. Do we then take responsibility for removing the excess, for returning the land to an equilibrium more in line with what went before? What point do we take as this 'before' – what came after?

What is the better course of action? What is more moral? What is more natural?

CAL FLYN

orty miles to the south, on 15 February, I am high on Cnoc Damh, the hill of the stag.

And well it might be, for we've been on the trail all day. Every time we lose sight of one band of deer, another comes along. The predator slink through the shadows is becoming second nature. I feel something has shifted in me, in my relationship to the deer and the land.

I woke in the loft of the empty house, listening to the wind scuffing over loose roof tiles. Then I felt *full*, sated almost. I was taking my place at the top of the food chain.

So clumsy, now, to put into words. It was a primal experience, a visceral one, in the true sense of the word.

Up here on the hill, with mud on my face and blood under my nails, I am far removed from reasoned debate. Questions of ownership, of quotas, seem impossibly distant: an abstraction in a solid world of cold water, of wet rock, of hunting on instinct.

As the others patiently scan the hillside for movement, I sit with my back against a rock mapped with lichen and look out across the glen. It is a huge empty space, through which air moves and bands of deer roam, herds that drift and shift in size and shape, like shoals of fish, or clouds.

Its surface is tufted with gold-stranded grass like a hand-tied rug, ornamented in the dim colours of peat moss and bell heather. Far off through a bluefish haze, the lone stone sentinels of Assynt stand in wait below an unhurried sky.

From high up, I can see how the face of the hillside is veined with striations worn by wandering ruminants, treading and retreading the paths of least resistance. Everywhere there is evidence of the perpetual pull of entropy, as the earth – loosely tethered – slips as willingly from the rock as slow-cooked flesh from the bone. Here and there peat hags rise from their beds, heads hairy with dead vegetation, their soupy black undersides dissolved by and dissolving in the low and constant rain.

For all its scale, this is a subdued, sleeping landscape, its most visible signs of life drained away over long winter months. Very occasionally the silence is interrupted by red grouse, who fly up gabbling at close range, scarlet brows the only flash of colour in a muted hillscape. That, and the ever-retreating backs of the red deer.

No people. No trees, either, of course.

This is the evidence: of the removal of predators, of the overgrazing of livestock, of the winter feeding of wild deer by gamekeepers seeking to keep their quarry alive for the season. This is the hand of man, writ large across the land. But who is to say that it is not beautiful?

I imagine the valley flooded by trees: a treeline rising up the sides as if it were a bath filling. Sproutlings coming up in a thick fur, searching the curves of the Earth. Soon metamorphosing into an endless forest of native woodland: Scots pine and silver birch and hazel and juniper. Wild flowers freed from their rocky ledges could grow wild in meadows and sunlit clearings – globe flowers, sow milk whistle, yellow bird's-nest, toothwort. The strains of songbirds on the air. What ecologists call 'structural diversity'. It is a good thing. I know.

But what of the austere eroticism of the disrobed hillside? The smooth sculptural curves of the mountains, of the bell-bottomed glens. The tributaries clefting rock like breasts. The soft puckering of the skin of the Earth, the folds and wrinkles. I see golden limbs, sprawled in slumber. I see trickling meltwater falling as rivulets of sweat from the brow; pooling in the navel of the land.

So many people, drawn to these places by the peculiarly raw aspect of their splendour, lose the ability to look at them through uncritical eyes. They become property in need of repair; habitats degraded by overgrazing, or compaction – of spoilt opportunity. They see only the goodness that has been leached from them.

One can know too much, I think.

Far below a speckling of silver lochans is strung together in a rosary by a single serpentine stream. Dim flat light radiates from surfaces of brushed steel. I feel doors opening within me. Lights flicker on in the dark. ∎

ALBERTO GIACOMETTI
*Very Small Figurine, c.*1937–1939
© THE ESTATE OF ALBERTO GIACOMETTI/LICENSED IN THE UK BY ACS AND DACS, LONDON 2017

SWIFTS

Adam Foulds

A fter twenty days the chick cracks its shell and breathes for the first time. Three days earlier, an older sibling had done the same so there is already a wobbling, hissing presence in the nest. There may be one more egg that is a further three days from hatching. If food is scarce, the new chick and its younger sibling will die as the parent birds focus on feeding the eldest, strongest bird, its head start in growth favouring it in the race to adulthood and thus making it most likely to survive. Fortunately, this season food is plentiful. The parents feed the chick pieces of a wadded mass of spiders and flying insects that they have caught in the air and stored in a hollow in their throats. (Later, the chick will consume the whole ball in one swallow.) The parents collect any faecal sacks that the chicks have produced. Mostly these are dropped away from the nest as they fly off to gather more food. Sometimes, for reasons unknown, they are swallowed, perhaps to appease for a moment the parent birds' own hunger, which must be frequently tormenting through the long weeks of rearing chicks.

After a few weeks of growth, the chick begins moving purposefully about the nest, exercising its flight muscles, the pectorals that power the downstroke and the supracoracoideus muscles that raise the wings again. There isn't room for the chick to open its wingspan so it performs a sort of press-up on its wing tips and vibrates its chest.

After several more weeks, the chick spends long periods sitting at the entrance to the nest, staring out at the world, learning in some way, calculating, calibrating. It does this for a few days, then flies out.

Fledging is not a graduated process for swifts. There is no hopping from branch to branch in short, bumbling flights that increase in height and distance. The swift leaves the odorous, parasite-infested darkness of the nest all at once and takes to the air where it may fly, may live, without touching another solid surface, for the next three years.

S wifts eat, sleep and mate in the air. They drink by catching in their mouths raindrops or the ice crystals of cloud vapour, the same way they catch the tiny airborne spiders that make up the greater part of their diet. Landing only in order to breed, adult birds fly continuously for ten months of the year, firstly in the skies of sub-Saharan Africa, then heading north across the desert on migration to their breeding sites across Europe.

Swifts come closer than any other creature to living in the sky and having air and ceaseless movement as their home. They reach great heights and great speeds. They can fly horizontally at nearly seventy miles per hour. Only the peregrine falcon flies faster than this, and then only in its brief vertical stoop, the arrowing free fall it uses to catch its prey. Swifts are small animals, about six and a half inches long with a wingspan of about two and a half times that. They typically breed after three years and die after seven or eight, though some have been known to live for more than twenty.

L innean name *Apus apus*, deriving from *a-pous*, 'without foot', an ancient Greek misconception about a bird that never seems to land.

Swifts do have feet but they have barely any muscle to support them so they must land on a vertical surface some distance from the ground if they are to take off again easily. If they do, through mischance, end up on the ground, they hop and tumble and flip as they struggle to get back up into the air.

I used to watch swifts landing and taking off. I became a birdwatcher aged about ten, a passion with a sudden onset, a new insatiable hunger to see and know this particular thing. Across the road from the playground of my primary school were the kind of pebble-dashed, semi-detached houses found all around outer London. In a few corners under their guttering, swifts had built their nests from feathers, paper, dry grass and seeds glued together with saliva. I stood by the railings at break time and watched. The landings looked like footage of an explosion played in reverse, a rapid, whirling motion sucked back into a small, sudden stillness. Hanging on to the walls afterwards, they looked stunned, incapable, decrepit even, a humiliating transformation after the dazzling athleticism of their flight. What a strange sensation that first landing must be for them, gripping something close and solid, the world's motion stopped after months if not years of wandering in the sky touching nothing except, very briefly, the trembling body of another swift to mate. When they took off again, to catch the air under their wings, they dipped down almost to the road's surface before climbing up in an arc and zooming away over roofs and out of sight. When they had landed, fixed to the wall, they were infuriatingly hard to see, each bird a little, narrow darkness, folded into itself. I wanted to be able to distinguish their features as I could with other common birds, with robins, blue tits, or blackbirds. I knew the faces and characters of those garden birds. Swifts were more elusive, wilder somehow.

Flying high and fast, swifts are usually apprehended in their whole shape, the narrow curved blade of the wings bisected by the compact, missile body and short, forked tail. Apart from a small patch of lighter plumage under their chins, usually invisible, swifts are a uniform dark brown, which against most skies reads as charcoal black, occasionally flashing silver when caught by the sun. Even in the midst of our cities, they are nature turned away from us, racing away, indifferent or averse. Melville's line about the whale comes to mind:

'Thou shalt see my back parts, my tail, he seems to say, but my face shall not be seen . . . I say again he has no face.' It is not surprising, given how the swift flickers at the edges of our perception, that it has accumulated none of the fond iconography that has attached to the swallow, an apparently similar bird. They are not in fact related; swifts are more closely related to hummingbirds. Swallows are everywhere – in graphic design, in the names of restaurants and boats, in book titles and tattoos. They are much more colourful than swifts with their elegant, evening-dress pattern of steel blue, white and scarlet, and exuberantly long tail streamers. They are more personable, flying lower to the ground and gathering in twittering groups on fences or telephone wires. But the difficulty swifts presented made me want to see them all the more. At home, I could use my binoculars, craning my neck to catch them in flight, turning the focusing wheel as fast as I could to make the image sharp. There were exhilarating moments of synchronisation when I would, as it were, ride with them, lifted into the air myself by the lenses' magnification, until I lost them behind a sudden treetop, blurred intervening brickwork or roof tiles. Or they would simply swerve too fast for me to follow.

Usually swifts are heard before they are seen. You hear the screaming and you look up. The sound is distinctive, thin, astringent, unphrased. When a number of swifts are screaming together, as they often do in the evenings, there seem to be two notes in it at an interval of a minor third, like the cuckoo's call. The sound arrives in Europe with the heat of summer, their screams descending through the burning clarity of blue skies. In my childhood memories, this harsh, alien note marks a key change in the season into a new intensity and weeks of prolonged heat and light. I know this recollection of cloudless and consistent summer weather can't be right but what comes back to me with the swift's scream is the dramatically heightened climate of so many novels – *The Great Gatsby*, *The Go-Between*, *The Cement Garden*. As a boy out birdwatching, I also unravelled a little in the heat, spending too long watching swifts flickering in the heights, hearing that cry, or looking for kestrels in trees whose leaves started to flame in my vision. Several times I got sunstroke and only realised too late when the symptoms manifested. Burnt, tender skin, nausea, a stunning headache formed out of black, heavy pulsing that worsened with movement; illumination, of a kind. This was how I learned the lesson that nature had power even in the south of England where it all seemed harmless, without venom or danger, contained within small woods and scrublands that were like large untended gardens. I learned that sunlight is radiation arriving through space and that there are forces at work that you cannot see.

Swifts, like many other birds, can perceive the Earth's magnetic field. Exactly how they perceive it is a matter of conjecture. Perhaps it is as a sensation, as we might feel heat or cold or the thickened, prickly air of static electricity. But given the connection between their eyes, magnetic-responsive molecules and the Cluster N nerves in their brains that process orientation, and how all of them meet in the thalamus that processes visual information, it is more likely swifts *see* the magnetic field as colour or intensity. Maybe it looks like the Northern Lights but fixed in place. This may make orientation easier to maintain on their long migration over the Sahara and the seas and when they rise to high altitudes at night to sleep as they fly.

Up there in the dark, under stars or clouds or in moonlight with a bright platform of cloud beneath them, flying continuously, swifts sleep with one half of their brain at a time. Because brain hemispheres are wired to the opposite eye, swifts close their right eye while the left side of their brain sleeps and vice versa, in cycles. Unihemispheric slow-wave sleep. The same method is used by beluga whales and some other marine mammals, also constantly moving in their fluid medium. At dawn, in the vast transformation of light that they must experience at that empty height – and that we occasionally glimpse through aeroplane windows – they descend again to where the air currents are speckled with flying food. At dusk, they ascend once more.

In a poem about being caught, in various ways, in an earthquake, William Empson repeats the line, 'The heart of standing is you cannot fly.'

Sometime between 1937 and 1939, Alberto Giacometti carved a tiny human figure out of plaster, now called *Very Small Figurine*. It stands no more than two inches high, almost half of which is made up by the plinth on which the figure stands. 'Plinth' is accurate but misleading. The figure does not seem to be raised above the ground in the familiar way of a statue but to stand flat on an excavated chunk of the Earth's surface. She is rooted in the position – feet together, arms by her sides – familiar from Giacometti's later, larger works and with hindsight she looks like their seed or embryo. She is barely thicker than a matchstick. Her exquisitely carved head and neck, the forms of her breasts, arms, hips and legs, are executed at what seems like the very limit of possible dexterity. One leans in to see her to discover exactly how much detail has been achieved.

Her tininess means that we look down at her as if from a great height, out of her sky, so to speak, as swifts might look at us if they had any interest, or like the gods. We look down and find in miniature exactly ourselves, our own predicament and rather than feeling like gods we feel our own lumbering impotence. There is something in the attitude of *Very Small Figurine*, isolated on her plinth, her chunk of Earth, that we pity, something incomplete, plaintive, petitioning, although at the same time she is resigned, she endures. She calls up to us in silence. We loom over her in that space from which it seems answers or aid might come but we have none. The human situation: to be upright, questioning, bearing the whole weight of our flesh and vertical skeleton on our feet, our intelligence, our self-consciousness finding in the space around us a distressing emptiness. Animals do not do this, which is one reason we are drawn to look at them. Acting always in the present, in continuity with their world, they create no abyss. We look at them to become absorbed in that state of immediacy, freed from the vertigo, the sickness of meaning.

The heart of standing is you cannot fly.

M y fascination with swifts and their aerial life is tangled up, I know, with several fantasies of escape from this human situation. One aspect I am looking up at with yearning is lightness, weightlessness. This is not a daydream of having the power of flight but of sharing the swifts' apparent escape from the force of gravity. It is gravity that over the years bends our backs, grinds down our knees and ankles, pulls our cheeks down into jowls and makes our skin hang. It is gravity that makes us groan when we get up out of chairs and that makes falling fatal for the elderly. Pressed down by gravity they cannot reach for help; they may be there for days, they may die there. The upright posture of Giacometti's *Very Small Figurine* is gravity borne with as much stoicism and grace as possible. A different art form, ballet, expends much effort to elaborate an image of the beauty of life with the constraints of gravity relaxed, its limitations overcome. Dancers leap and leap again into the air, attempting to 'hang' there. They step as if floating on the very tips of their toes, on a single toe. Gravity exacts its price in injuries, sprains, fractures and deformities. A ballerina can usually sustain only a short career.

In 1810 Heinrich von Kleist wrote 'On the Marionette Theatre', an extraordinary and unique essay fiction about humans and their bodies, movement and self-consciousness and our 'fallen' state. In it, a Mr C, a former dancer at the opera, explains why he finds marionettes superior to human performers:

These marionettes have another advantage. They haven't discovered the law of gravity. They know nothing about the inertia of matter . . . The force that pulls them into the air is stronger, more powerful than that which shackles them to the earth . . . These marionettes, like fairies, use the earth only as a point of departure; they return to it only to renew the flight of their limbs with a momentary pause.

I think of swifts in their endless, unquenchable flight. And I remember that at the end of a performance in a miniature theatre, marionettes, like swifts at nightfall, are pulled upwards out of sight.

I know that a swift's movement is compulsory, that its life is one of unending hunger and necessity. There is no real envy in my mesmerised attention, my fascination with their other way of inhabiting the world. They are pared down, honed into that elegance and thrilling speed by the fine margins of survival. I think of the young swift entering its third year in the sky, still months away from landing for the first time since it dropped out of the nest and caught the air under its narrow wings. I follow it out along that knife-edge as far as I can.

Let's say she is a female. In the sky, she will find a mate and they will remain paired for the rest of their lives. He will find a nest site, shooting past possible locations and 'banging' them with his wings to see if they are already inhabited. He may end up having to fight for a place, quick, scrambling conflicts in which he leans back and claws at his opponent with his feet. The pair build a cup-shaped nest, gluing the collected material together with their thick saliva that sets hard. They have mated – moments of quick, precise contact in the air – and eggs have formed inside her. She lays two or three in the nest. After they have hatched, she and the male spend all their time gathering food for the chicks. She flies over five hundred miles a day doing this, filling her throat with flying insects and returning again and again to the sudden gaping mouths. She tries to avoid wasps and other stinging insects but if other food is scarce she will collect these too. If all goes well, after weeks of this effort, at least one of the chicks will leave the nest and join the adult birds in their home in the air before starting the long journey south back to Africa.

A problem with nature writing, both for the writer and reader, is that it ends, the miniature theatre closes, and we move on. This imparts the satisfying sensation of something completed but it falsifies the dynamics of the living world in which nothing is finished and everything is flowing, including us. As you read this now, swifts are flying. When they are far from your mind, when you are fast asleep tonight, swifts will be flying. ■

NOTICEBOARD

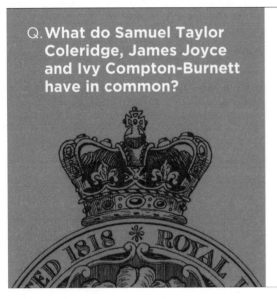

ANIMAL STUDIES

Elliot Ross

Introduction by Alexander MacLeod

W hat exactly are we looking at?
The title of this series of photographs is *Animal Studies*, but I am not sure about that second word. A noun or a verb? A thing or an action? Are these studies *of* animals or are these *animals studying*?

My wife likes the squirrel the best. 'He's coming right at you,' she says. 'That is full-frontal squirrel and he is not backing down.' My kids, maybe inspired by the game, think that all the birds really are angry, and, to me, it seems the orangutan is weary and he has seen this all before.

When I look at these images now, for maybe the thirtieth time, I barely see the animals any more. All of their amazing bodies are still there, of course, and it should not be possible to ignore this kind of variety – the astounding shapes that life can take – but I have to admit, after my first and second journeys through this pile, it wasn't the feathers or the fur that brought me back to the beginning again and held me here for so long.

Owl to orangutan, hyena and squirrel; start with your monkeys, end with the pigeon – it does not matter. What I have called a hyena could just as easily be some kind of leopard. I cannot tell you where the line is supposed to go between the monkeys and the orangutan. Even two kinds of owl move beyond my capacity for secure classification. All I know is that somebody else seems to know. Somewhere out there, there are other people, zoologists and taxonomists, and they can give names – accurate, specific names to all of this – and detailed descriptions to match their various purposes.

For me, though, for me, right now, none of that is important. Sorry Linnaeus. Your kingdoms, your phyla, your genera, your species, even your most basic domains need not apply. Because when I look at these images all I see are the eyes, the intensity of the staring, and somehow it is always the same. All of these thoughtful creatures, all of them so full of thoughts, all of them engaged in this basic business of putting the world together.

But what exactly are they thinking about as they study this man who seems to be studying them?

It is hard to tell where I fit in this exchange or even who I am supposed to be. Am I, are we, the subject in these pictures? Are we the ones looking in? Or, through Elliot Ross, do we become the object the animal studies? Probably, as always, it is some mysterious combination of the two. ∎

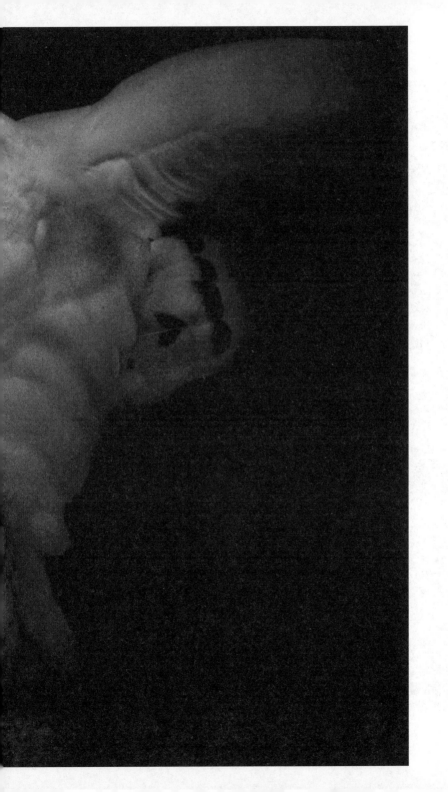

Dorothea Lasky

Snakes

Serpents are a holy green

Halos on the bottom of the earth

Very slittering creatures

But there is a spirit to things

What is a snake and why is it important?

Imperial feminism

The medical profession

You should be speaking at my funeral, kid

Healing is not shameful

There is no shame in healing

There is no shame in getting better

All those healthy children

The time in-between

When you feel that poetry is the last thing you need

That's the time you need poetry most of all

Time is fierce

Pussyfoot doggerel

Fierce winds of it

In this life

There is always time

To make a comeback

Said I, the poets, with their branding

Oh write what you are, poets

Everyone's a snake

Most of all, including you

You have to steel yourself

From the garden

Be who you are poets

Cold creatures

With no other thought

But to thrive, then kill

THE FARMER'S SON

John Connell

Beginnings

I'm twenty-nine and I've never delivered a calf myself. But that's all about to change because I've got my arms in her passage and I'm trying to find the new calf's feet.

As a farmer's son, I've birthed calves aplenty, but always as the helper, holding a cow's tail up or pulling the calf out at the last moment. My father has been in charge of the calving for twenty-five years and when he wasn't my brother took over, but now it's me.

I'm home again in rural Ireland, back from being an immigrant, here to write a novel, to try and make it as a writer and, in exchange for a roof over my head, it's been agreed that I will help out on the farm. There's a lot tied up in this birth for me, much more than the cow knows.

The red cow moves suddenly and lets me know her strength and power. I must be quick. I must get the ropes around the calf's feet, slide them above the hock and pull them tight. The amniotic fluids wet my hands, my arms, and I remember now the talk I have heard other men say, that your hand gets weak after a time, that the clasp of her vaginal embrace takes the power from it. I must be quick lest the calf die.

I grasp the first foot and slip the rope over his hock.

I have the other foot. I take the second rope from the side of the gate and slide it onto the calf's leg, it slips and falls and I curse and now I think perhaps I do need help, but it is too late. To wait might mean death and then I would be called a fool for trying on my own and there would be a huge row. No, I must focus. The cow has nearly finished the nuts I gave her to keep her calm. When they are gone she will remember her distress and begin to thrash and kick again and then the job will be all the harder.

I stoop low, take the rope and turn to my work again. The rope is now on the second foot. I pull gently, but the calf is big: he will not come like this, I will need the jack. I take the mechanical wench, placing it on the cow's hips, and hook the ropes into the slots and begin to winch.

I must do this right I tell myself, but I have seen it done so many times I know my actions. I must jack, then lever down to bring the calf out. The biggest pull will be his head, and once I have that out the rest should follow, except the hips which can sometimes be trouble. I winch the jack five times and hear the sprocket chime out in the quiet shed. I pull down and as I do the cow bellows low in a noise I don't recognise, a noise of pain and strangeness.

'There, there,' I say, clucking to her. I let off the pressure and jack once more and feel the sprockets turn and the ratchet move up the teeth. The legs emerge more fully now, but still no head and so I lever down again and I can see his nose and it looks so flat, perhaps his head is squashed. The cow bellows low again and I feel her feet tremble.

'Don't go down on me,' I say to her and let the pressure off once more and she stands to again and we repeat our chores. Her contractions push the calf as much as she can, but he is beyond contractions now, for he is too big and our job is at a point where it cannot be undone.

I jack once more and the cow roars.

I pray or at least I think I do.

The head emerges and I have no time to thank God, for I must jack with all my might and keep going for the cow could give way and if she goes down, the calf might die. I see his tongue wag and I know he is alive and I pull still stronger now though my arm is growing tired. I jack and jack and he is emerging now, fluid and strong, and he is red like his mother with a white sketch on his face. He is the son of our stock bull of that I am sure, for I can see the old bull's face in his.

Horns

The weather has not improved. There was talk that February would be better, but then the snows came and that talk ended.

Da has not been out on the farm for a week for he has had a bad cold and I have run the place myself. It has been a busy week and I am tired, for between the days and nights I am but a servant to the cows. Sometimes I have wondered what is it all for. I do not earn money at this work and the farm pays for itself and no more. To make a living at farming is hard work and there are few full-time farmers in the area, most men have other jobs as builders or tradesmen or teachers. Da is one of the few full-time farmers, but that was not always so. For more than two decades he also was a builder with my Uncle John, but he retired ten years ago for the work had grown too hard and though he was still young it had aged him.

Today is Da's first day back on the farm. The first batch of this year's crop of calves are getting older now and we must burn off their horns. Dehorning the cows is a requirement from the Department of Agriculture, for the meat factories will not take a horned beast.

We burn the calves' horns now to save sawing them off when they are older. We use a gas torch to heat a small metal bowl that cuts the horns from their heads. It is sore for the calf, but it is better done now than to wait, for to saw the horns off a weanling is a bloody job: the horn must be cut at the root to stop further growth.

There are twelve calves to be treated today. We lock them in their pen and set up our calf crush, which is a small metal box. Da brings his equipment out and sets it up on the wall of the calf bed area.

'Grab that first calf,' he says.

I wrestle the first of the crop, taking him by the tail and ear and steer him towards the crush. I must keep close quarters, for though the calves are small, a kick in the right place could hurt me.

Da lowers the torch towards the calf's head. It cries for its mother as the hot metal pierces its flesh, he shits himself and squirms in the crush. I whisper soft words and tell him it will be over soon. I see my father scoop up the small piece of horn contained in the torch.

'Just one to go,' he says and bends to once more.

The calf cries out again and then it is over.

'Next one, Johnny.'

I can tell that he is in a good mood now, for he only calls me Johnny when things are going well. I nod and grab another calf and we repeat the process.

The last calf escapes my arms and I hear Da cluck. He is growing tired.

'Ah, will ya catch him!' he says, irritated.

'I'm bloody trying,' I say, and I can hear now our tones change.

When we finish he does not speak and we drift apart once more, tempers cooling. We have done well not to fight. I inspect our work. The calves are sore but they will thank us in the long run.

Bloat

In the shed this morning a lamb that has always been somewhat poorly is lying out. He is foaming from the mouth and panting. His gut is swollen and large and I do not know what is wrong. Dad will not know what to do, for we have only had sheep these past three years and it is to me he looks for insight into these beasts.

The lamb's mother paws the ground in an effort to make him stand, but he will not rise. I set him upright but after a few steps he collapses once more. When I squeeze his gut, there seems to be air, a huge quantity of it stuck inside him. It is some form of bloat, that much I piece together. To be a farmer is to be a student forever, for each day brings something new.

I walk inside to get some vegetable oil and baking soda to quell the bacteria in his gut.

'Got a lamb with bloat,' I say.

Mam and Da are sitting in the kitchen.

'Swollen as big as a balloon,' I say.

I must stomach-tube the mixture to him. The article I Googled has said that natural yoghurt will also work. I grab some from the fridge and return outside with my home remedy.

He is panting heavier now and I worry it is too late and that he may die. I do not know how long he has been this way. Perhaps I missed him in my rounds. Perhaps Da did too.

I insert the slender plastic stomach tube down his throat and carefully attach the syringe full of fluid. If I get this wrong I will send the fluid to his lungs and kill him. He squirms and cries and I hold him tight. I push and inject the fluid.

The article tells me that a few minutes after inserting the stomach tube I should insert a second tube made of rubber down his throat to allow the gas in his stomach to escape. I must massage his belly and gently force the air from him. I let the lamb recover and take a moment to settle myself. They say farming has changed, that it has become industrial and mechanised, but still if the farmer has not the nature to care for his beasts when sick they will die. I have known the hardest of men to be soft and gentle with their animals in a way they never are with their own families.

Settled now, I insert the tube once more, and rub and massage his distended belly; I hear the rift of gas and smile, for the operation is working. He is still swollen but perhaps less so now. I massage and rub and shake him for ten minutes or more.

I think I am finished now, for I can hear no more air coming out. I must isolate him from his mother, for her milk will only feed the bacteria growing in his stomach, and that needs to be killed. He must fast and then I will reintroduce healthy bacteria through the natural yoghurt.

It will be twenty-four hours before I know if I have succeeded. The article tells me that in extreme cases a needle should be inserted through the abdomen into the stomach for an emergency release of the gas. I am not confident enough to do this yet and it would cost fifty euros to take him to the vet, more than the lamb is worth. I must take my chances. If he has not improved in a few hours I will intervene and perform the emergency operation.

I have had good luck with the lambs this year so far. I have lost few and those that have died have died of causes that man could not prevent. There was the lamb taken from me by his mother's carelessness, for she lay on top of him and smothered him in the night. Then there was the lamb who was born a triplet and a cripple. Da said it was from the way he had lain in the womb, for his neck was forever bent to one side and he could not stand upright.

I have lost no calves and for that I am the most thankful. Mam jokes that we have St Francis working on overtime at the moment. Let not the saints get tired, nor the older gods. We will pray to whatever keeps luck alive.

At 2 a.m., I waken and do my rounds. I check the lamb and find him standing upright. He is brighter now and cries out to me for food. His stomach is still swollen, but he seems not to be in pain. The lamb roars to me and I agree that yes you can eat. I give him some natural yoghurt and then make a small bottle of milk replacer and feed him childlike in my arms.

'You're a good lad,' I say and rub his head.

The stock exchange

He has died in the night. The foam had come back, it was around his mouth and still wet. His body was stiff and cold.

I know now that I should have performed the emergency needle operation. I had been too much of a coward to do it and now he is dead. It is my fault.

Da is not sympathetic when I tell him about the lamb and says it was never fuckin' right in the first place. I tell him of the needle and the ifs and buts, but it is pointless now.

I take a needle and perform the operation on his lifeless body so I will know how to do this next time. I pierce the flesh in his abdomen where I imagine his stomach is. I feel the metal push through the layers and then the gas escapes and his body deflates. It was this easy. I am a fool.

I place his stiff body in the empty fertiliser bag and I will discard it later. I am annoyed and disappointed. I am reminded of a neighbour's saying: where there's livestock, there's deadstock. The phrase helps but does not bring back the lamb. ∎

In the warm, womb-like space of the cottage, the light from the open fire flickers and casts dull shadows of birds across the wall. On my gloved hand, a slender, lightweight and beautifully patterned female sparrowhawk. To my left, a smaller but no less impressive male. Both hawks emanate a quiet, self-contained calm. A fine balance of precision and coiled unsparing instinct, all contained within a gossamer skein of feather, skin, muscle and bone. They remind me of that thin slither of a moment just before a jack-in-the-box pops. Months ago these hawks arrived, via a vet, from the wild, injured. To have them legally in my possession is a rare pleasure.

It is not commonly known, but hawks smell.

On arrival their breath was a mixture of metallic sour fish and ammonia, a rancid, tacky odour that remained on the skin and in the nose. Having spent several weeks nursing them back to full health, their rehabilitation is now complete. Consequently their lungs, throat and stomach emit a scent as nuanced and complex as a six-month-old breastfed baby.

A second, more subtle smell rises from their feathers. All hawks have a protective sheen, a bloom, weatherproofing against the rain. A healthy hawk's bloom has a low musty tang, rotting peaches, the marmalade mossiness of dried twigs. The scent is one of pure nature. A fresh bloom on a hawk with perfect feathers is divine. Anything that smells this good is undeniably fit and ready to go free.

Having come from the wild, and not been captive, bred or purchased, these hawks are perhaps the most important I have ever owned. They are utterly irreplaceable, priceless in a very literal sense, and I cannot wait to set them free.

I hope I never see them again. ∎

ko ko thett

Swine

Like a pageant sow the pregnant moon has lowered herself to rub her spine against a pine limb.

If you dream of horses you will have to travel far. If you are in a town under a cavalry siege, your dreams surely will be equine.

If you dream of pigs you will remain where you are. The back garden of my childhood home was too small for a horse.

It was a pigpen. Pigs are enlightened winged horses. You don't mount a Pegasus the way you mount a pig.

I rode bareback, I rode out all the revolutions.

Each time a young swine was castrated, all hell broke loose. When balls rolled, blood went everywhere.

The only Master I got to know was the young Master, whose speciality was swine sterilization.

Hooves still ruffle my feathers – hundreds of hoofs on gravel roar like tanks rolling at the Battle of The Vale of Tears.

In the post-apocalyptic world,
only winged horses shall remain.

I am not so sure about that.

Once, he landed briefly on the kitchen scales when I was baking. He weighed less than half a cup of sugar. How could someone so small be so much?

It's years since he died but it's always this bird I'm asked about, this one who exercises fascination, as if there was some truth in the superstitions surrounding magpies and in this random connection, there could have been the key to a mystery of kinds. It's almost as if he might have been frightening. The only thing that was, was the knowledge of his intellect.

Our connection was random – he fell out of a tree and I picked him up. It was the usual bargain: freedom or death. He lived five times or so longer than he would have done in the wild. I can't know if the bargain felt worth it for him.

He was of notable beauty, but they all are. One of his feathers, black and iridescent blue, still turns on a thread in the warmth above the lamp on my desk.

His life was one of calculation and endeavour, of learning and watching, remembering and trying. He could be aggressive. He measured thoughtfully, practised speech with precise and prolonged dedication. Once when I wept, he flew to me, huddled against me, muttering softly.

It still seems vaguely seditious or presumptuous to write these things of another species. Why? Because we have so little belief in the consciousness or capabilities of others?

By now, I'm used to what people say and think about magpies – the shallow judgements, the uninformed questions about destruction and cruelty, asked by members of the species which best knows about destruction and cruelty.

The images I keep are of him flying up the long stairwell of this tall house, vanishing into a column of sunlight; him flying down from his favourite place on top of the kitchen cupboard to stand on the pages of the book I was reading as if demanding to be read. We'd stay quiet, just like that, looking at one another for a long time. Perhaps we were both pondering the chasm of the separation of our worlds or perhaps only I was.

I still miss him. The moment, the years, could never be repeated – there could be no possibility of replacing him. I wouldn't want it anyway.

I hear and see magpies every day. They're everywhere, in the air, in sound, talking, whispering, calling with his voice. They must be as capable as he was of things unimaginable, of empathy and grace, reminding us of what's beyond our knowing. ■

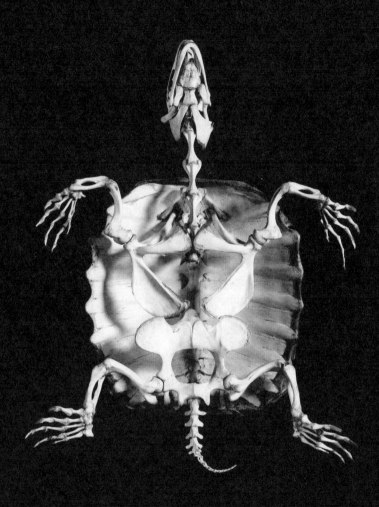

Tortue molle, Chitra indica, 2007
from the photobook *Évolution* (Éditions Xavier Barral)

LOGGERHEADS

Rebecca Giggs

I believe, against the data, that the summers of my childhood were hotter. If pressed I will concede I only remember the weather *felt* worse, that its frustrations seemed greater, and that this has little to do with what meteorological instruments record. How we weather the seasons in our bodies and buildings is what comes back to us, not the recorded temperature of the days. What I remember is this: in Perth in 1991 you could run a hand across the fibro walls of our primary-school classroom and notice the metal struts within still radiating heat from *yesterday's* sun.

At the beginning of last year – on an afternoon when over a fifth of the country darkened to wine-red in the Bureau's schematics, indicating temperatures of above forty degrees Celsius (104 degrees Fahrenheit) – I sat in air conditioning and found it was not hard to ignore the weather of the future. Things were bad enough already. A schoolmate's toddler had been rushed to Emergency having stumbled barefoot off the grass onto a metal manhole cover. I heard he had partial-thickness burns. Blackouts rolled through the western suburbs of Sydney as the grid crashed. On televised maps a streak south of the Australian centre keeled towards purple, a colour that had only been added to the range in 2013 to indicate temperatures above fifty-two (126 degrees Fahrenheit).

It helped to lie to yourself and think: *no one lives out there.*
Meanwhile, an ABC News 24 reporter surveyed a beach in
Queensland and pointed to piles of what looked like soft grenades
or little kids' shoes, abandoned tread-side up. These were dead turtle
hatchlings, surfaced from clutches buried months earlier by their sea-
bound mothers.

'Loggerheads,' the reporter said in a neutral tone, 'have cooked in
this terminal sand.'

I went into the faculty kitchenette, turned on the tap and waited
for water heated by the pipes to run cold over my forearms. *Terminal
sand.*

What idiom or instrument captures how the weather is felt by
the animals, in their bodies, their nests and niches? The planet's
atmosphere was never more quantified or monitored, but the uneven
sensitivities of other species to the weather seem too alien, too interior
and multiple to measure or articulate. Hard to picture, let alone
describe, the way the summer is experienced by organisms arrayed
with senses dissimilar to our own.

I want to suggest that this problem is like asking, 'How do animals
experience pain?' But it is not *like* that question. Very often it is exactly
that question.

'Weather,' writes the anthropologist Tim Ingold, 'is not perceived,
but is the atmospherics of perception.' Ingold is most right, I think,
apropos of heat. Lacking the visible theatre of snowfall or rain, heat
stupefies and narrows the temper. Heat summons haze in everyday
car parks, distorting parts of objects that touch or detach. Meddling
with ways of seeing and states of mind, heat heightens attention
to smaller, effortful labours. Heat dehydrates, forces squinting,
stipples the skin with sweat or scorches it. When Ingold refers to
'the atmospherics of perception', my guess is that these are the sorts
of things to which he is referring. Heat is intimate. Heat generates
surprising intimacies with others, as when, for example, you find
yourself discussing sleep and sleeplessness with strangers.

A scaly creature basks in the same weather as us, but in different atmospherics of perception. Schoolbooks still teach that reptiles belong to the category 'cold-blooded'. A misnomer. Ectotherms internalise the temperature – their metabolism is sped on by the sun. Our human vocabulary seems inadequate to evoke the anguish of a reptile when it's seared in its surroundings. Lacking the physiology to pant, perspire or otherwise shed temperature, turtles, reptiles, can only seek shelter. Their blood runs hot and hotter without it. Sea turtles (as the tortoises in fables) are slow on land and clumsier flippering through the sand. The rookery on Mon Repos beach looked mercilessly exposed.

I pitied the loggerheads, but as tap water overflowed my cupped hands, my attachment to their distress felt far-fetched. Anything to which we can compare life in an incendiary turtleshell, any notion we have of that infernal experience, belongs, I think, on a list of the ways hell is dreamt and suffered. Which is to say, the analogy is not of this world. Our only point of reference is existence, implausibly, *post*-biology.

More preoccupying than the turtles, though, in that minute standing over the sink, was something I had been trying to explain earlier about a remedy for heat stress. This was the trick I nightly swore by: you got a few handkerchiefs, bandanas, or any bits of fabric really, and soaked and froze them. Then you tied the strips around your wrists and neck to chill the radial arteries and jugular veins running up to the head. The reason it worked had something to do with returning colder blood to the heart and the brain. Those organs being most in charge of regulating the body's internal thermostat, you wanted to cool them first, in turn to pacify the rest of the body. I had been going to bed during the heatwave in this lucidly scientific way – with bits of frigid cloth wrapped around my throat and cuffs, sprawled on a mattress stripped of all linen.

The associate professor in the elevator said, 'What I'm wondering is, wouldn't that *constrict* the veins? Isn't this why the body naturally flushes – increased blood flow to the skin? What you want is to increase blood flow in hot weather.' She popped the lid off her insulated cup and examined the inside. 'Trapped heat. In your head? That'll keep you awake, no question.' Her own sleep was unfazed by the weather, though she slept, she added, in a town house with climate control.

This conversation had thrilled me. In the corridors I often heard the phrase 'the human condition' uttered – without irony! – but how rarely we talked about the animals we were in Arts. Mammal to mammal. We held in common our physical senses, our apparatus of perception, but although we experienced the same weather, we assimilated it differently in our bodies and in the places where we lived. And this whole business of the head as an impoundment where heat might become imprisoned: it sounded vaguely Ayurvedic. Reminiscent of the medieval humours, which once you might have used leeches to treat, drawing off instabilities of bile, blood and phlegm. Wasn't that somehow about the weather too? I distantly recalled reading that malignancies of the humours were connected to the seasons, to peregrinations of weather inside of the body.

Through the kitchen window clouds were beginning to heap. Being heat fatigued you could readily believe in impossible truths. Like, even an average cloud weighs as much as a Boeing 747. Against the way technology has rendered 'the cloud' – a generic metaphor for the dispersed, electrical no-place – these actual clouds were glamorous, specific and finite. I saw a formation of clouds that will never be repeated throughout history. I saw that formation from an angle and at a moment in time nobody else did. The brightening blackening of their cores. Out of every window in the building, and all across the city, anyone who looked up shared in that prerogative: to claim to witness something that wouldn't be repeated, the sky, that instant, from there, amassing. The idea that formed in our heads was everywhere alike.

Storm, we willed. A wish that was an atmosphere, palpable as a pressure front. Please, please, please. *A storm.*

The question *what will happen with the weather* is the central question of our age. Furnished by precision meteorological instruments and long-range computer modelling, our best international science describes weather systems changing in unprecedented, wildly variant, ways. A hundred-and-twenty-three temperature records are broken in fewer days – purple is added to the Australian heat index. A further category of bushfire risk is authorised, the official upper limit now 'catastrophic' above 'extreme'. The weather works on editing its own phrasebook, striking through defunct terms and demanding new ones. Rubbed out of this lexicon for good is the meteorological *force majeure*. Act of God. ∎

Early one morning in the month of June, someone ran over a huge black rooster on County Road W in Wisconsin hill country. Thirteen years old and punch-pleased on an X-90 minibike bought for me by my godfather, I arrived on scene at sunrise with the body still warm, not yet stiff when I kicked at it with the toe of my work boot. Usually I was the only one who passed by so early on this country road, driving over to the Thompson farm, where I helped with chores in the barn at dawn. Perhaps Weasel did it, the older Slama boy, out all night, speeding home drunk. Three upraised black feathers fluttered in the breeze at a right angle to the body, weakly flagging Weasel to slow down for God's sake – the rooster's last gesture.

The rooster belonged to Weasel's dad, who raised goats, rabbits, sheep, one donkey, and a flock of these oversized black chickens, running loose on the bare-dirt lawn of his eyesore house just around the curve. *Fuck you* to the neighbouring Lutheran farmers said the toppling house, the junker car in the drive, the chickens getting onto the road. One of the neighbours had called the county about the donkey, saying it wasn't fed.

Driving past the Slama place I throttled down, vividly aware that Kristal Slama slept behind those upstairs windows, though I did not know which one. I closed my eyes and kissed the air. The fine-grained skin around her eyes had a purplish tinge, as if she had great sorrows, though just my thirteen years old.

Behind the Slamas' house a little copse of birch and scrub oak and maple grew on a hill. Woods that are pastured are prettiest of all, because grass grows under the trees where the cattle have trampled the brush – the cattle acting as nature's gardeners. On two or three evenings I saw Kristal sitting in the copse with a book in her hands, a runaway, I thought. She made no gesture, and each time I promised myself that I would stop and speak to her if she appeared again. I remember just at that curve the sweet and heavy stench of the rooster's rotting flesh, softening and sinking into the tarmac, just a splash of tallow by summer's end. In the autumn, the vagabond Slamas moved away. ∎

WEB

Joy Williams

'**X**enotransplanting,' the rat repeated. 'That's some ugly mouthful.'

'Oh they're very excited about it,' the horse said moodily. 'They say it's a real game-changer with little risk to society.' He was an entire horse – not a day went by that he didn't thank his lucky stars for that – but he was a nihilist too, although an anxious one.

'Everything's a game to them and the game is making them crazy,' the rat said. His name was Victor. All the rats were called Victor after the ubiquitous trap. A bit of black humor came down through the generations.

'Wilhelmina will be spared,' the horse said. 'That's the good news. The bad news is that her offspring will be genetically edited to become reliable if unwilling organ donors. Your heirs, Victor, will be genetically programmed to suffer only as usual.'

'Whatya mean?' Victor said. 'I want them to enjoy a proper lifestyle. Kitchens. Dumps. Fairs.'

'No more fairs,' the horse said. 'They're going to schools. Probably not Harvard.'

'Why not Harvard!' Victor said, insulted.

'Maybe Duke,' the horse said.

'Pray that they don't go to Tulane,' the sheep said. 'Isn't that where those unfortunate monkeys went? Very badly handled.'

'The spinal cord does not regenerate,' one of the spiders said. 'You'd think they'd have learned that by now.'

Wilhelmina trotted into the barnyard. She was Some Pig. Her eggs easily incorporated the human genetic code. All her piglets were star patents. But she often worried about their lack of engaging pigness – they looked a little blank to her. They had these disturbing one-yard stares.

'Your issue will be increasingly engineered with specific maladies, Victor,' the horse went on. 'Tumors, leukemia, Alzheimer's . . .'

'Something akin to Alzheimer's surely,' one of the spiders said. Charlotte's children possessed her looks and intelligence but sadly not her creativity. They were widely traveled though they made very careless webs. This was not entirely their fault, however, as environmental factors were no longer conducive to their inherent skills.

'. . . enlarged prostates,' the horse concluded wearily.

'No one wants leaner or tastier meat from us anymore,' the sheep said. 'Or rather they want that too but they particularly want our organs – our sister pigs' hearts especially. They're having more and more difficulty with their own hearts so they want ours.'

'But our hearts belong to us most of all, don't they?' Wilhelmina said.

'It's taking the eyes, our beautiful eyes, that is so distressing,' the sheep said.

'Xenografts,' one of the spiders said. She thought she'd spell it out but then thought, oh why bother.

'I feel faint,' Wilhelmina said.

'Wilbur cozied up to the humans too much,' Victor said. 'That's why we're in this mess.'

'It was those buttermilk baths and being wheeled around in the baby carriage,' the sheep said. 'Wilbur was a little . . . how shall I put it . . .'

'That Charlotte was a piece of work though,' Victor said. 'What a gloomy broad. Remember those lullabies?'

' "Sleep, sleep, my love, my only / Deep, deep, in the dung and the dark; Be not afraid and be not lonely!" ' Wilhelmina murmured.

'Yeah,' Victor said.

The others looked shyly at Paul and Priscilla, the silent calves who had been cloned from the meat of their butchered mothers.

'I prefer the Tennyson poem,' the sheep said. 'I find it more hopeful. May I?'

Victor smirked. She was one affected ewe, always pretending she was from the Emerald Isle and just visiting this barnyard.

The sheep began:

O yet we trust that somehow good
   Will be the final goal of ill,
   To pangs of nature, sins of will,
Defects of doubt, and taints of blood;

That nothing walks with aimless feet;
   That not one life shall be destroyed,
   Or cast as rubbish to the void,
When God hath made the pile complete;

Paul and Priscilla turned away, like ghosts.

'I feel so sorry for those kids,' the goose said.

'What does he mean by pile?' the horse asked. 'Pile seems a rather careless choice.'

'Just rhyming, don't worry about it,' Victor said. 'Remember the fish story? When Charlotte caught the fish?'

'But it's not the pile that rhymes, it's the feet with complete. Do you think he meant . . .'

'It was her cousin who caught the fish,' the goose said.

'Whatever. What's a fish doing jumping up and getting caught in a spiderweb in the first place? Was it a salmon? All those PCBs make them kind of weird. There was something wrong with that fish.'

'Charlotte was exercising poetic license,' one of the spiders said.

'Speaking of stories did you know that Ludwig Wittgenstein was reading *Black Beauty* when he died?'

'Really?' the horse said.

'I don't know if he was in fact reading it, but they say it was on his bedside table.'

'A wonderful book,' the horse said. 'It promoted kindness and sympathy and the worth of all creatures.'

Kindness, sympathy and love, one of the spiders mused. Without them man is nothing. Perhaps . . . ? She looked at her sisters entombing a fly. But it would take so long to compose this sentiment in separate webs and didn't the pest control service come at the end of each month?

'Nobody writes books like *Black Beauty* anymore,' the horse said.

'I hate to tell you kid,' Victor said, 'but you were never in this book either, the one you think you're in now.'

'I am,' the horse said morosely.

'It's a dream kid. You don't exist.'

'But I do,' the horse said.

'You were collected running free on the great lands of the American West, dumped in a corral and trucked off to the slaughterhouse.'

'Oh it was awful, awful,' the horse said trembling. 'But what did we do to warrant such horror?'

'You ate grass didn't you,' Victor said. 'You were taking up space.'

'This is all so frightfully depressing,' Wilhelmina said.

'At least your little ones are respected symbolically,' the goose said to the sheep. 'Not that it matters in the end of course.'

'Yes yes,' the sheep said fretfully. 'Symbolically we feel quite honored, well somewhat honored.'

'Our creaturely kingdom is being slaughtered daily, hourly, without a qualm on their part. And now we will be sacrificed for even more extreme adventures,' the horse said. 'They are the brutes of the cosmos.'

'Won't the children save us?' Wilhelmina said. 'Won't the children stand up for us?'

'I dunno,' Victor said. 'They seem a little distracted. Or hypnotized or something. Always staring into those white screens.'

'I simply can't believe the things I've heard and that we are discussing this very moment,' the sheep said. 'It's simply too insane and totally unwarranted.'

'Are they not thinking?' Wilhelmina said. 'I don't think they're thinking.'

'I was once told that if people acted as certain insects do they'd possess a higher intelligence than they do at present,' one of the spiders said.

'It's all illusory,' another spider said. 'Maya.'

'I fear it really isn't,' the horse said.

'I wish I had that name,' said the third spider.

'Why don't you then!' Wilhelmina exclaimed. 'You can. Why don't we forget all this gloomy talk and have a naming day for . . . MAYA . . .'

No one responded, not even the little spider who didn't have a name.

'This is the life we've been given and our children as well,' the sheep said, 'but why do they take it away so cruelly and with such horrible fascination and delight?'

'Some say that if they didn't utilize us, murder us for this and that, they wouldn't allow us to be at all,' the goose said.

'But wouldn't they miss us?' Wilhelmina said.

'I don't think they would. They'd find a way around missing us,' the horse said.

'They're so clever,' the sheep said.

Victor loudly burped.

Be not afraid and be not lonely, Wilhelmina thought, but couldn't bring herself to say it. She wanted to reflect on her pretty piglets but night had fallen and she and her friends were once again hopelessly caught up in trying to comprehend the terrible ways of men. ∎

CONTRIBUTORS

Nadeem Aslam was born in Pakistan and now lives in England. He is the author of five novels, most recently *The Golden Legend.*

Ned Beauman is the author of four novels, most recently *Madness Is Better than Defeat.* He was named one of *Granta*'s Best of Young British Novelists in 2013.

John Connell is a writer, journalist and farmer from rural Ireland. His memoir, *The Cow Book*, from which 'The Farmer's Son' is taken, will be published by Granta Books in the UK in 2018 and by Houghton Mifflin Harcourt in the US in 2019.

Diane Cook is the author of the story collection *Man V. Nature*, a finalist for the 2015 *Guardian* First Book Award and the 2014 *Los Angeles Times* Art Seidenbaum Award for First Fiction. She was a producer for the radio show *This American Life* and is the recipient of a 2016 fellowship from the National Endowment for the Arts. She lives in Brooklyn.

Ben Crane is a falconer, writer and artist. He has travelled the globe researching and learning about falconry. He currently lives deep in the Shropshire countryside with his hawk and two dogs.

Emily Critchley is the author of *Ten Thousand Things* and a book of selected writing, *Love / All That / & OK.* She is the editor of *Out of Everywhere 2: Linguistically Innovative Poetry by Women in North America & the UK* and is Senior Lecturer in English and Creative Writing at the University of Greenwich.

Steven Dunn is the author of *Potted Meat.* He was born and raised in West Virginia and, after spending ten years in the US Navy, he earned a BA in reative writing from the University of Denver. 'The Taxidermy Museum' is an extract from his new novel, *water & power*, forthcoming from Tarpaulin Sky Press.

Cal Flyn is a writer from the Highlands of Scotland. She has worked as a reporter for the *Sunday Times* and the *Telegraph*, and in 2017 she received a John Heygate Award for Travel Writing from the Society of Authors. Her first book, *Thicker Than Water*, was published in 2016.

Adam Foulds is a poet and novelist. He was named one of *Granta*'s Best of Young British Novelists in 2013 and the Poetry Society's Next Generation Poets in 2014. His new novel, *Dream Sequence*, will be published in 2019.

Sam Garrett has translated over thirty books from the Dutch. His translations include *The Evenings* by Gerard Reve, *The Dinner* by Herman Koch and Tim Krabbé's *The Rider.*

Rebecca Giggs writes about ecology and environmental imagination, animals, landscape, politics and memory. Her essays and stories have appeared in *The Best Australian Science Writing, The Best Australian Essays, Meanjin* and the *Monthly*. She teaches at Macquarie University in Sydney. Her first book is forthcoming from Scribe.

Arnon Grunberg is a Dutch novelist and reporter. His work includes *Tirza, Silent Extras* and *Blue Mondays*. He lives in New York.

Cormac James's most recent novel is *The Surfacing*. His short fiction has appeared in *AGNI, Guernica* and the *Dublin Review*. Born in Ireland, he now lives in Montpellier, France.

Britta Jaschinski is a German photographer based in London. Her work has been published and exhibited worldwide and received numerous awards. In 2017 she was named the GDT European Wildlife Photographer of the Year, and won the BigPicture Natural World Competition Grand Prize. She is the co-founder of the group Photographers Against Wildlife Crime, together with editor and writer Keith Wilson.

Dorothea Lasky is the author of five books of poems, most recently *Milk*. She is currently an assistant professor of poetry at Columbia University's School of the Arts.

Ben Lasman's fiction has been published or is forthcoming in *Tin House, Wired, ZYZZYVA* and the *Other Stories* podcast. He lives in New York and has recently completed a novel.

Alexander MacLeod's first book of stories, *Light Lifting*, won the 2011 Margaret and John Savage First Book Award and was a finalist for the 2011 Frank O'Connor International Short Story Award, the 2010 Scotiabank Giller Prize, and many others.

Christina Wood Martinez is the assistant editor at Dorothy, a publishing project. Her fiction has appeared or is forthcoming in the *Virginia Quarterly Review*, the *Sewanee Review*, the *Literary Review* and *Puerto del Sol*.

Margaret Mitsutani was born in Pittsburgh, Pennsylvania, in 1953. She has lived in Japan since the 1970s and has translated work by, among others, Kenzaburo Oe, Mitsuyo Kakuta and Kyoko Hayashi.

Daniyal Mueenuddin is the author of the short-story collection *In Other Rooms, Other Wonders*. He lives in Lahore, Pakistan, with his wife and son. Kristal Slama is the protagonist of his forthcoming novel, *No Loving Cup Tonight*.

Adam Nicolson is the author of several books about history, writing and the environment, including *Sea Room, Power and Glory, Gentry* and *The Mighty Dead*. He is currently writing a book on the year Coleridge and Wordsworth spent together in the Quantock Hills, and another on life between the tides.

CONTRIBUTORS

DBC Pierre was raised in Mexico and became a visual artist before turning his hand to writing. His first novel, *Vernon God Little*, won the 2003 Man Booker Prize. At work on a fourth novel, he divides his time between the UK and Ireland.

Elliot Ross is an American photographer. His work has been exhibited internationally and is featured in collections in the US and abroad.

Christine Schutt is the author of two collections of stories and the novels *Prosperous Friends, Florida,* a 2004 National Book Award finalist, and *All Souls,* a finalist for the 2009 Pulitzer Prize for Fiction. *Pure Hollywood and Other Stories* will be published in May 2018.

Aman Sethi is a journalist living in New Delhi and the author of *A Free Man.*

Helge Skodvin is a Norwegian photographer. *A Moveable Beast* was a finalist for the 2016 Magnum Photography Award.

Yoko Tawada is the author of many books, including *Memoirs of a Polar Bear.* She writes in Japanese and German and has won the 1993 Akutagawa Prize, the 2016 Kleist Prize and the 2017 Warwick Prize for Women in Translation. 'The Last Children of Tokyo' is taken from her new novel with the same title, forthcoming from Portobello Books in the UK. It will be published as *The Emissary* by New Directions in the US.

ko ko thett is the author of *The Burden of Being Burmese.* 'Swine' is taken from his forthcoming poetry collection, *Bamboophobia.*

Joy Williams is the author of four novels, four story collections and the book of essays *Ill Nature.* She has been nominated for the National Book Award, the Pulitzer Prize and the National Book Critics Circle Award. She lives in Tucson, Arizona, and Laramie, Wyoming.

Esther Woolfson is the author of *Corvus: A Life With Birds.* She has been artist in residence at the Aberdeen Centre for Environmental Sustainability and writer in residence at the Hexham Book Festival. An Honorary Fellow in the Department of Anthropology at the University of Aberdeen, she is currently working on a new book about human attitudes towards the natural world.

Evie Wyld is the author of *After the Fire, A Still Small Voice* and *All the Birds, Singing,* plus the graphic memoir *Everything Is Teeth.* She lives in south London where she helps run Review, an independent bookshop. She was named one of *Granta*'s Best of Young British Novelists in 2013.

Nell Zink grew up in rural Virginia. Her books include *The Wallcreeper, Mislaid* and *Private Novelist,* and her writing has appeared in *n+1* and *Harper's.* She lives near Berlin, Germany.